THE SPIDER:
HELL'S SALES MANAGER

THE MASTER OF MEN! SPIDER®

HELL'S SALES MANAGER

By Grant Stockbridge

POPULAR PUBLICATIONS • 2024

CHAPTER 1
MARKED FOR DEATH

I T WAS a dead-end alley, squeezed between the high brick walls of two apartment buildings—dark as a buried coffin. Then the light came, like a white sword, reaching for the figure who crouched there in the darkness, and the man behind the flashlight gasped.

He heard the indrawn breaths of his two companions as the black-caped figure whirled, showing a predatory, beak-like nose and fanged, protruding teeth beneath the floppy brim of a large, down-turned black hat.

That much the three men behind the torch saw in the first glimpse. One of them choked on a curse, and another cried out in a high, strained voice that was little more than a whisper.

"The Spider!" he gasped. *"It's the Spider!"*—and their three guns turned that narrow alleyway into a hell of screaming lead!

But the man they called the Spider was already in swift motion. His forward leap made the long cape bell out behind him enormously, filling the alley from wall to wall. Behind that cover, he swayed his body aside like a swordsman avoiding a lunge. The first three bullets plucked through the middle of the cape, and so missed him. Then the Spider was whirling, slapping his right hand across his chest. His left arm swept the cape aside—and his own black automatic spat answering lead.

There was the crack of breaking glass, and a man out in the

1

Then the sinister bald-headed
creature in red… vanished!

street swore harshly—and there was darkness once more in the crevasse of death. The leaden breath of the Spider's single bullet had blown out the light!

Those three gunmen shrank aside from the mouth of the alley, and their faces were white; there was a frightened shine to their eyes. No human being could have dodged their fire; yet the Spider had. No human being could have fired so accurately into that dazzle of light; yet the Spider had. It was the thought of that unerring accuracy, of the dread reputation of the man they had caged in the alley, that made them flatten now against the wall beside its mouth. Their breathing was fast and deep, as if they had run violently for a long way.

"He's only a man," one of them whispered. "Let's take him!"

Another laughed, and cursed. "Maybe, but he kills guys like us. He puts that nasty little red seal on their foreheads... after they're dead!"

"He's just another crook," the leader whispered back. "Like any other crook. This bunk about his killing only to help people, that's plain nuts. He's got a racket of his own!"

"Maybe...."

From the darkness, laughter sounded thinly. It seemed to whisper in their very ears, to fill all the night, yet it was not loud. It was flat, metallic and penetrating, and it was full of mocking menace. It was the laughter of the Spider!

One of the men shrank back from the alley. He began to walk rapidly down the street.

"Come back, Mike—you fool!" the leader whispered. "We got to get this guy, or the chief will get us!"

"Yes, Mike," whispered the Spider's mocking voice. "Come back! Come back... *and die!*"

THOSE THREE men at the alley's mouth, murder guns in their fists, crouched down fearfully in the protection of the brick walls... but they did not flee. Desperation was white in their faces. One of them twisted his gun around the corner and began to shoot again....

In the darkness, the Spider—who in another life was known as Richard Wentworth, wealthy clubman and amateur criminologist—crouched low to the cement floor of the alley and estimated his chances. They would see him if he lifted himself high enough to swarm up the fire escape above his head. And those three shot straight! Any lesser man than the Spider would already be stretched dead upon the pavement.

Out in the street, the three men were whispering together again, and the alley funneled their voices to the Spider's listening ears.

"We don't have to take him!" said the leader. "All we got to do is hold him here until the police come. Somebody is sure to have phoned for them already. Soon as the sirens get close, we beat it see? And we got the Spider!"

Wentworth smiled grimly in the darkness that sheltered him. It was a simple plan—but unless he moved swiftly now, it would work!

His eyes ranged upward over the fire escape that lifted above him from the level of the first floor windows, which were barred. That fire escape was his only chance, at present, the only means of escape except the mouth of the alley, where three men with guns waited.

Mike leaned gingerly forward to peer into the alley. "I can't see anything. Maybe he got away, Hank."

The leader, Hank, shook his head. "No way out except the fire escape, and I been watching! No, we got him, and—"

"Look!" Mike yelled. "Look, he jumped for the fire escape! Now we got *him!*"

Mike's gun blasted an exclamation point to his cry and, suddenly, Hank and the third man were on their feet. And Mike was right. Swinging from the fire escape was a black-caped figure!

"Give it to him!" Hank snarled.

Their guns rolled thunder down the narrow abyss. For a moment, under that brutal fusillade, the figure in cape and hat swung below the fire escape—and then it dropped back into darkness again. There was the clattering sound of shoes striking the pavement, of a body thudding to earth!

And at that moment the sirens of the police began to whimper faintly in the distance.

But in the alley there was silence.

HANK STOOD motionless, the gun ready in his fist. Mike tugged at his arm. "Come on, Hank. We got no time. The cops—"

Hank grunted, "All right. Get Al."

Mike reached out and touched the third man on the arm, motioned down the street, and the three of them, shoulders hunched, crowding close together, sped along the pavement. At the corner, they paused for an instant where the streetlight spilled its ghostly pool of light. They paused, and then ducked out of sight. The sirens were much louder.

A few windows racketed upward, and frightened faces of men peered out, now that the danger was past. When the police cars whined to a halt, someone shouted, "In that alley! That little alley! Three guys shot the Spider in there! I heard them say so!"

The police swore and darted toward the mouth of that alley. They produced guns and flashlights, and then they laid the brilliance of their torches against the darkness and peered along the abyss. There was nothing, absolutely nothing in the alley. There was not even a blood-stain. It was fortunate that, for those few seconds, they did not think to look upward—fortunate for the Spider.

With only those few seconds to spare, he made the last rungs of the ladder and swung himself to the roof. He stood there then, breathing easily. The violence of that dash to the roof had not even quickened his breath. With swift, methodical fingers he unknotted a length of silken line which was tied to his two automatics, so as to form a coat-hanger for his cape and hat. He smiled grimly at the welter of bullet holes that had pierced both hat and cape. Lucky for the Spider that, instead of daring their lead himself, he had merely pulled up cape and hat at the other end of the silken line, as if it were the Spider himself who swung upward to the fire escape!

It had been touch-and-go there in the alleyway, but his mind had already left the memory of it behind. His whole thought now was concentrated on the apartment of William Hackett, on the top floor of this building; William Hackett, who had dared to offer testimony against Waxy Matthews, the crooked politician, and therefore was doomed!

It was to protect that courageous witness that the Spider walked tonight. Yet already a new fear was forming in Wentworth's mind as the hunched figure glided, silent as a black shadow, across the roof. For it was a curious thing that the crashing of guns in that narrow alley had not brought Hackett's police guard to the window! The other police would be investigating that fact in a few minutes. He must work fast....

Seconds later, he had looped his fabulous silken line over a chimney, and was lowering himself gently over the edge beside the window of Hackett's apartment. He had no fears of the line breaking, though it was little more than the thickness of a pencil. This line, woven of the highest grade silk, had a tensile strength of a thousand pounds! The police knew it well. They called it the Spider's Web! With his shoulders twisted beneath the black drape of the cape, dangling by that slender cord, Wentworth did strangely resemble the creature whose name he bore. No spider could have been more silent....

BESIDE THE window of Hackett's apartment, Wentworth hesitated until his eyes could stab through into the dim interior. He was peering into a bedroom and, beyond, a door opened onto a lighted chamber. His gloved hands flitted over the casement, eased it open without a sound. He ducked in quickly, lowered the window on the silken strands to hold them ready for emergency exit. Motionless, he stood then while ears and nostrils tested the air of the apartment.

There was no sound at all.

No sound, but Wentworth's nostrils thinned and his mouth grew straight and hard, for there was a curious scent in the air. It was a sickening smell—the odor of burned human flesh!

Two long silent bounds took Wentworth across the bedroom. His cape whipped out from his shoulders, and there was a fearful promise in the forward thrust of those shoulders, in the steadiness of the two fists that now gripped the butts of twin automatics! Through that doorway into the light—and Wentworth froze!

There was another man in the room, but he represented no menace to the Spider; and no danger could ever touch that man again. He was William Hackett, and he was dead.

Even Wentworth's eyes, which had gazed on death so often, and death in awful forms, tightened when they examined Hackett's corpse. If this was a gangster murder, it was a curious business. On Hackett's forehead was a puckered burn. He had been branded there, and the wound showed purplish against the dead, yellow flesh; a cross within a circle like a four-spoked wheel. That in itself was horror enough, but it was the way the man had died that shook Wentworth. Hackett's head was crazily misshapen. It looked as if it had been squeezed on the sides, so that it had bulged forward to meet that awful branding iron. But there were no abrasions or bruises on the sides of the man's head. Somehow, the touch of that fierce branding iron, *had pulled Hackett's frontal bone forward until his skull was like an orange that a man has stepped upon!*

Wentworth shook himself free of the paralysis of horror that gripped him, and there was a cold anger in his heart. This man had dared to do his civic duty, and this was the result! Waxy Matthews sought by this means to escape the just penalty of his misdeeds! Wentworth's lips became bitter, tightened the line of his chiseled face. Waxy might evade the law by this means; in fact, he had—the moment Hackett died! But the Spider dealt in another sort of law! Wentworth looked down at the twin guns in his fists, and a slow and ominous smile moved his lips. It was not a pleasant expression!

He pivoted on his heel, and his eyes swept over the room. The overcoat and uniform cap of a policeman lay on a chair by the door, but the guard himself was not in sight. A dozen swift strides exposed the entire apartment. The guard was not in the suite at all, unless… Wentworth stared at the door of the closet beside the front entrance. In a long bound he reached it, opened it gently, shoulder braced against the wood. Just a crack of two inches—then he jammed it shut again!

Then Wentworth faced about, and the fire that smouldered in his gray-blue eyes was an awful thing to see. In that instant he heard shouts in the building; the police were on the way up. That meant all the lower floor exits were guarded. Wentworth's eyes swung toward the window by which he had entered. No more he could do now, not here. His business was at the hideout of Waxy Matthews! Wentworth had taken two strides toward the window when he saw his escape rope snake down across the glass; saw the two ends, which he had left as a loop, snap down through the darkness. His escape to the roof had been discovered and destroyed! And no policeman could fail to recognize that silken line; could fail to know that the Spider was in Hackett's apartment!

THE FROWN that crossed Wentworth's forehead was more of annoyance than fear. Every second was precious now. He had to get to Matthews fast, for it was the swiftness with which his justice struck, as well as the deadly certainty of his small red seal, which made him so feared throughout the Underworld.

Wentworth started toward the front door, then shook his head. He smiled slightly and took off his black hat, thrust it under his vest. He took the length of severed silken line and fastened it to the knob of the closet door. He glanced about him and was ready. He picked up the telephone from a table by the front door and rapidly spun the dial. He leaned his shoulders against the wall, carelessly, phone to his ear. He could hear men soft-footing along the hall now; could hear cautious calls from the roof. They were tightening the net for the Spider....

Wentworth's face softened, and the smile on his lips was suddenly gentle when he heard the voice over the wire. "Hello, Nita, sweet," he murmured, and his eyes were happy. It was always like this when he heard the voice of the one woman in the world who knew his perilous secret, the one woman who had that right—Nita van Sloan, whom he loved. "No, nothing serious, dear," he said, "but I'm afraid that little errand I mentioned will take longer than I had thought. I may be late for our dinner engagement. I might even miss it altogether!" Just beside him, he heard the knob of the door turn cautiously, but he had already ascertained that it was locked. He heard the grunt as pressure was put on the panel. His voice lowered. "It's nice of you to wait dear, but you'd better have something to nibble on while you wait. And Nita"—his voice grew very grave—"guard yourself!"

"Open up, Spider!" came a policeman's voice. "We got you cornered!" A gun butt pounded on the door.

"No, no, that's nothing," Wentworth said easily into the phone. "Just some rather peremptory gentlemen who want to get in. Yes, the police… I'm looking forward to dinner, dear."

A heavy blow made the door shudder, and Wentworth saw that the facing which held the lock's slot was loose.

"Goodbye," he murmured, "and take care of yourself!"

He replaced the receiver, and a gun blasted a hole beside the lock. Wentworth smiled, and flicked off the lights… It was perhaps a minute later that the door crashed violently inward. Light streamed across the room, and a mass of policemen wedged in through the entrance. Guns glinted in their fists, and the ceiling light flicked on suddenly.

"Holy Joseph!" whispered a policeman. "Look at Hackett! *What's happened to his head?*"

The men stood rigidly, staring at the corpse. That was why none of them saw a silken line jerk strongly at the knob of the closet door. They heard the latch rattle, heard the creak of the hinges. As one man, they pivoted. Guns raked upward… and they did nothing. They only stared. A body was pitching forward out of the closet. Good God in heaven, *two bodies in the closet!*

They fell forward, those two murdered men, with a slow weariness, as if being crowded in that narrow closet had tired them. Their knees clumped on the floor, and the first corpse, a big man in shirtsleeves, with his blue police trousers rolled a little. He thudded down on his back, and his left arm flung out wide. There was a bullet hole in his forehead. The second man pitched straight forward. His head struck the dead cop's stom-

ach, and a sound between a whistle and a moan emitted from that stiffening throat.

From the doorway, a man gulped.

"Jeez, oh jeez!" he moaned. "I'm going to get the chief!"

His feet were staggering a little as he pivoted and began to run heavily along the hallway. The sergeant in charge said slowly, "Yeah, call the inspector."

No one looked after the man who ran along the hallway, or noticed that his trousers were dark gray instead of blue, like the police overcoat he wore. It was only after a while that the sergeant jerked up his head.

He said, "Hey, where's the Spider?"

They scattered through the apartment, and they found no one. The sergeant glared at his men, and then a puzzled look came over his face.

"Say," he rasped. "Somebody went for the inspector. Somebody left, but, by God, the whole squad's here! Somebody in a police uniform… Damn it to hell, this dead cop's coat and cap are gone! *It was the Spider!*"

They rushed wildly through the building then. They shouted from the windows, but it was pretty late. Wentworth had a three-minute start. But they found the dead cop's overcoat and hat. It was laid neatly across the hood of the inspector's car, and in the dust on the windshield, there was scrawled one single word:

"Thanks!"

Below it, there was a glimmering red thing, a mark displaying hairy legs and poison fangs—*the seal of the Spider!*

But the Spider... had vanished!

CHAPTER 2
DEATH LIGHTNING

I F ANY of the police noticed a sleek foreign limousine that glided quietly along an adjacent street, none of them sought to challenge the car. The man behind the wheel had a strong, honest face beneath the peak of his chauffeur's cap, and the owner lounged comfortably against the cushions, a mildly bored look upon his chiseled, rugged features. A cigarette dangled from his fingers.

"It looks, Jackson," he said softly to the chauffeur, "as if the police were having trouble again!"

Jackson's broad jaws widened in a grin. "I hear reports the Spider was seen around here," he said. "Lies, of course."

The two men smiled quietly: Richard Wentworth in his own identity again; Jackson, who had served him in the army and afterward as his top-sergeant.

"To Miss Nita's now, sir?" Jackson asked quietly.

Wentworth's smile squeezed off his lips. "Downtown, Jackson," he said crisply, "and as fast as you can without attracting attention. We've got to beat the police to Waxy Matthews, though I'm not sure he's the guilty man!"

Jackson twisted his head about as he braked at a red light. "But you said Hackett was murdered, sir!"

Wentworth nodded slowly. There was grimness about his mouth. "He was murdered, yes," he said, "but as I told you, there were two dead men in that closet The police guard—and the man Matthews sent to kill Hackett!"

"I don't get that, sir," Jackson said slowly. The car was rolling again, its powerful motor muttering deeply as it sped through the night. "If Sniper, Waxy Matthews' ace gunman, was in the closet with the dead policeman, then he couldn't have been the one who killed Hackett and the cop."

Wentworth said, "Exactly. So Matthews ordered Hackett killed, as I had heard. And someone else beat him to the job!" His hand lifted, unconsciously, to a gun beneath his arm. He took it out deliberately and checked its loading, grimly replaced it. "Only one meaning there, Jackson. A new and horrible weapon of death; and a man who dares to slap one of our biggest gangsters in the face by killing his star gunman...."

"A new enemy, sir," Jackson said steadily. His voice was harsh.

"A new enemy," Wentworth acknowledged, "and the trail leads to Waxy Matthews tonight!"

It was a trail that must be followed at breakneck speed, and yet he had been forced to take the time to strip off the disguise of the Spider and resume his own identity for the dash downtown. Richard Wentworth was the personal friend of Stanley

15

Kirkpatrick, Commissioner of Police; but the Spider was Kirk-patrick's personal enemy! And friendship would never turn the stern Scots-Irish commissioner from the rigid execution of his duty. His suspicions turned with harassing frequency toward Wentworth... No, Dick could not afford to have the Spider seen riding in a car everyone knew to be Wentworth's.

WENTWORTH'S EYES raked ahead toward the apartment building in whose duplex penthouse he hoped to find Waxy Matthews. Matthews would have various bodyguards about him, men accustomed to murder... It was time to don again the habiliments of the grim avenger of the night! Wentworth dropped his hand to the edge of the left half of the seat, pressed a concealed button. When it slid forward, he drew out a fat briefcase that was made, actually, of paper. It was a neat package for the garb of the Spider, which he would don in the dark reaches of the night before entering the apartment building. There was a time when he had put on the disguise at leisure in the car; but no more. The danger was too great!

At the curb, the long limousine hesitated an instant—and a shadow merged with the darkness along the building wall. When the car rounded the corner, picking up speed for the dash home, there was no longer a passenger in the rear! The brightly lighted doorway of the apartment where Waxy Matthews lived did not darken to any trespasser; the guard at the steel door of the service entrance was not alarmed. But Matthews, secure in his long, successful defiance of the law, had not thought it necessary to place guards also in the building next door, a building only two stories lower than his penthouse. Presently, on the roof

16

of that shorter edifice, a crouching shadow moved....

At the base of the blank wall that led upward to the penthouse terrace, that shadow paused for a moment... and then glided straight upward! It was a climb that would have daunted many trained gymnasts, yet the upward drift of that shadow was effortless and smooth—and soundless! And presently a face, sinister beneath the broad black brim of the hat, peered over the balustrade of Matthews' terrace. The silken line was looped over a raised brick buttress. A vertical climb of thirty feet, yet the Spider's breath was unhurried....

It was while he clung there, his cape swirling slowly in the thrust of the cold winter wind from the river, that the thing happened. There was a rolling clap of thunder! A startled curse leaped to Wentworth's lips. Thunder, in winter time, with the skies crisp with stars? Impossible—yet the sound was identical. Furthermore, it was close!

In a smooth movement, the Spider cleared the balustrade. As he raced forward, he coiled his silken web in his hands, thrust it into a pocket of the cape. Once before he had been spotted by the Web. If he needed it to escape, it would take only seconds to loop it again over the buttress. His big guns leaped into his gloved hands as he raced silently across the terrace. Clean yellow patterns of light, from the French doors that opened out of the drawing room, lay upon the tiles. No moving shadows threw themselves across it; and after that thunder clap, there was no sound at all. Yet Matthews surrounded himself always with bodyguards! Where were they now?

Wentworth was almost abreast of the doors before he noticed a curious thing. The portieres inside were stirring as though in a breeze, but those doors were closed! It was only then that Wentworth saw there was no single pane of glass in any one of the door lattices. Every piece had been plucked out clean, as if by a violent explosion. Yet there were no glittering shards on the terrace. Instead, the glass was all inside!

That much Wentworth determined before he removed his hat so that he could peer cautiously inside. He swore and stepped squarely in front of the doors, for he knew now why there was no movement and no more sound within that room; why Matthews' bodyguards had not appeared! They were there, the bodyguards, seven of them. They lay squarely in the center of the room amid the wreckage of all its furnishings, and, looking at them, Wentworth felt nausea kick at his stomach. It looked as if, simultaneously, those men had been thrown together in the middle of the room. It looked as if, simultaneously, an explosion had taken place… *inside of each man!*

FOR JUST that split-second, Wentworth poised there on the brink of horror, and then bitterness drew his mouth in a knife-slit across his face. In a single movement, he wrenched open the doors and went bounding across this room of death. He was certain that this carnage could not have been wrought by that muted thunderclap he heard. He had been staring toward the doors when he heard it, and at that time the glass was already broken. Only one possible interpretation: The monster who had done this thing was still in the penthouse!

It is doubtful if any other man alive would have dashed in to meet a killer possessed of such an awful weapon. But the Spider was no ordinary man. Dreaded by the Underworld, misunderstood by the very people he served, he nevertheless was given a homage that amounted almost to reverence. In whispers, the people called him… *Master of Men!*

Three long bounds took Wentworth across the carnage of the drawing room. He went through the arched doorway beyond, and into the hall. He strode purposefully toward the room at the corridor's end—the room which he knew to be the office of Waxy Matthews. Suddenly, there was bright white light before him; suddenly, a man stood in the doorway! Then Wentworth's pace was arrested.

Was it a man?

The figure, surrounded by that flickering bluish halo of light, seemed incredibly tall. If it had arms, they were not visible, for a blazing red robe cased it from shoulders to the floor. The head was a bald gleaming knob, and the face… the face had no expression at all. It was completely calm, the cheeks smoothly contoured, the mouth set in a straight line. Only the eyes seemed alive. They… *blazed!*

Wentworth flung himself against the wall, and his twin guns jerked upward into line. His fingers were ready on the triggers, and he prepared to load that gaunt, mad figure with lead… The man in the red robe had not moved. His lips did not move

19

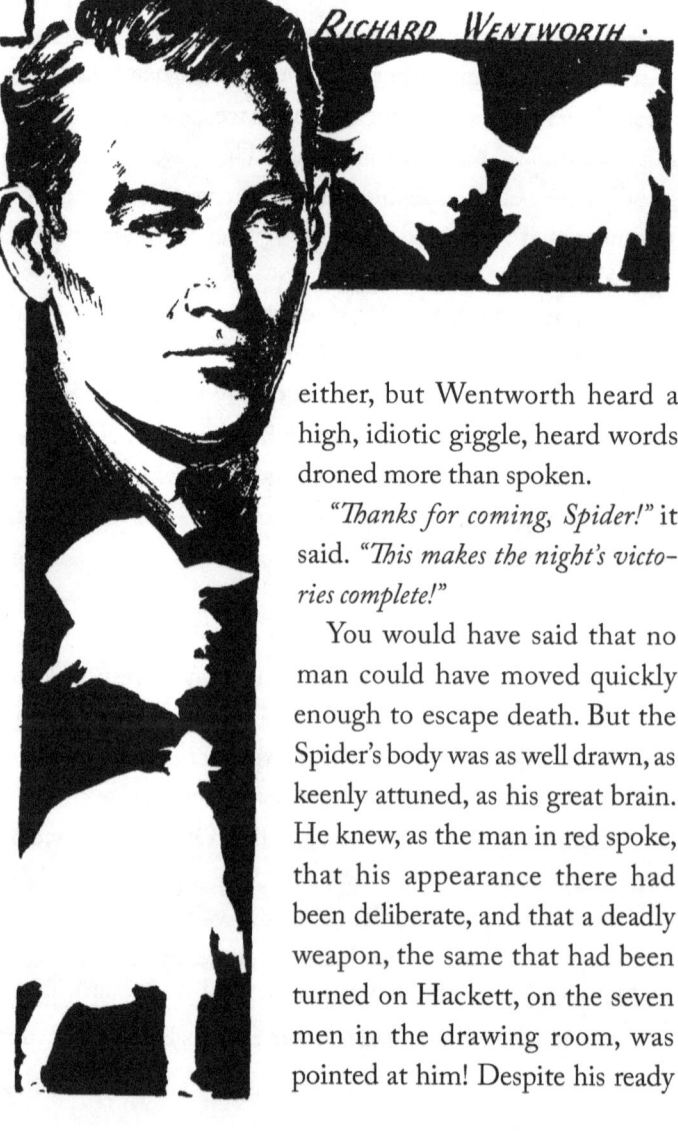

RICHARD WENTWORTH

either, but Wentworth heard a high, idiotic giggle, heard words droned more than spoken.

"Thanks for coming, Spider!" it said. *"This makes the night's victories complete!"*

You would have said that no man could have moved quickly enough to escape death. But the Spider's body was as well drawn, as keenly attuned, as his great brain. He knew, as the man in red spoke, that his appearance there had been deliberate, and that a deadly weapon, the same that had been turned on Hackett, on the seven men in the drawing room, was pointed at him! Despite his ready guns, Wentworth did the only thing possible. One instant, he was standing braced against the wall; the next he was plunging, horizontally, toward the floor. It was in the same split-second that he saw the lightning.

A small blue-white point of flame leapt from the folds of that red robe toward Wentworth. He saw that point prolong itself into a sword-like streak. It came while Wentworth was still in the air, falling, starting to squeeze the triggers of his ready, unerring guns. Suddenly, they were wrenched from his hands! He saw them flick upward past his strained, taut face. His hat and the black wig of the Spider, were wrenched from his head, and he was conscious of searing, incredible heat. His whole body seemed to linger in midair for a long, long instant before he plummeted to the floor! He could hear nothing at all. There had been a strain on his eyeballs that almost plucked them from his head, and he could not see. He knew that warm, salty blood was gushing from his nostrils.

THE SPIDER should have been dead. Only the fact that he had been falling at the instant the lightning struck had saved him. The momentum of his falling body had fought against the incredible power of that awful weapon. He should have been dead; his brain was in a black fog. Yet, suddenly, the Spider was

on his feet! The incredible will of the Master of Men pulled him to his feet. And he charged toward the man in red!

Blood streamed from his nostrils. There was a glassy stare in his eyes, and his black flaring cape, which kited back from his shoulders, was alive with tiny running flames! His empty, weaponless hands reached out before him, and from his wide-strained mouth there came an incredible sound. It was flat and mocking, and it stabbed the air like a dagger.

The Spider, blind, deaf, out on his feet save for the superb command of his will, charged empty-handed into the face of certain death—*and the Spider laughed!*

For an instant, the man in red stood motionless amid the dying blue flicker of the light. His expressionless face did not change, but his eyes changed. Their blaze of triumph became uncertain, and another light came into their shallow depths. It was a shine of superstitious fright!

With a small, strangled curse, the man in red whirled aside from the Spider's path. In two long strides, he reached the door of the penthouse and whipped through it. The jar of the closing door shivered through the walls, through the floor, and Wentworth felt it. He checked his race, turned blindly. He took three faltering steps, and his outstretched hands met the wall. The stiffening went out of his body, and he sagged against the wall, pressed his forehead against the cool surface.

From the streets below came a thin, persistent wailing. Sirens. The police were coming, and Wentworth, though he knew they would come eventually, had no warning; he could not hear at all!

Presently the devouring flames that crept up his cape sent

their painful messages to his brain. He stirred then, heavily, stripped off the cape, and let it droop from his fingers. He stared at it and realized his vision was returning. He stooped laboriously to pull the silken line from the inner pocket and hold it in his hand. He might need the line any minute. He took a few fumbling steps toward the door from which the man in red had appeared. He rattled the knob deliberately, then frowned. He could not hear a sound. How was he going to know when the police were at hand?

Wentworth shook his head, and moved on toward the office. At that moment, the sirens were at their loudest in the street outside. As Wentworth stepped across the threshold of the office, the sirens died out. The police had arrived!

But Wentworth stood there, staring at the shambles of the office. On the floor lay the corpse of Waxy Matthews, with that brand upon his misshapen head. There was a gun in his fist, but it was plain he had never had a chance to use it. Across the office from him, the magnificent mahogany desk had been wrecked. From the way the rug was rumpled, it was quite apparent that that heavy piece of furniture had been dragged violently across the floor—and apparently the door of the massive safe set in the wall had leaped to meet it halfway!

One thing was entirely clear: the door of the safe had been *pulled* from its sockets! Afterward, the safe had been looted!

THESE THINGS Wentworth saw in a single flashing glance, and his gaze, his reawakening mind, centered on the body of Waxy Matthews. In his death-clenched fist there was a crumpled slip of paper. Wentworth bent toward it with narrowing eyes. It read:

Received of Waxy Matthews, fee for elimination of witness, Wm. Hackett.

And the signature was a crudely drawn replica of the mark that had been branded on Matthews' forehead!

Wentworth smothered an oath. It was not that the death of Matthews, or his hireling gunmen, was any great loss to humanity. As long as the man in red, the Brand, confined his murders to criminals, it would not concern the Spider. But no man knew better than he that this was the standard procedure of the criminals who aimed at domination of the Underworld—and the conquest of humanity! Terror first must be spread among the hireling crooks the Brand must enslave, and then a frontal attack upon society itself!

How terrible that attack would be, Wentworth could testify! A new and incredibly powerful weapon had been used against him. The life had almost been torn from his body—*by a stroke that missed!*

Abruptly, Wentworth's eyes snapped up from his grim contemplation of the destruction-swept room. Through the floor beneath his feet, he had caught a faint vibration. He strained his ears, and they were still useless! He crouched and pressed sensitive fingers against the floor, and his face grew keen and wary. The vibration was slight, but each successive one fell in rhythm, and was a little more marked. No need even to guess at the meaning. That slow and cautious jar was made by the footsteps of a man… a man who crept furtively toward where Wentworth crouched!

Wentworth's hand whipped to an underarm holster, and it was only then he realized how severe had been the shock which had hammered him to the floor. He had forgotten to recover the automatics wrenched from his hand by the Brand's fantastic weapon! He remembered the gun in the dead Matthews' hand, but before he could whirl toward it, there was movement in the doorway. A man leaped into sight, and his mouth was stretched wide in a shout. He was one of Waxy's guards, miraculously recovered. He thrust forward a heavy automatic and, at a range of less than three yards, began to pump bullets straight at the Spider!

Death was blazing into the Spider's face, and it was death also that flamed in his gray-blue eyes. Incredible that any man alive could dodge lead flung at such close range, but there were times when the Spider seemed more than human. With a side-leap like a flicker of light he dodged, and before the killer could overcome his weapon's recoil to shift its aim, the Spider struck!

His left hand flicked forward, and it still held the coils of his silken Web. Like a many-thonged whip, it cracked into the killer's face and blinded him. In the same instant, Wentworth was diving headlong into the face of death! The gun blasted twice more, just beside Wentworth's cheek, and the concussion made him reel. His first blow glanced off the gunman's jaw. Even so, its force lifted the man's heels from the floor and slammed him against the wall. His gun-hand sagged. Wentworth poised for the knockout—and the man dropped to his knees, thrust the gun out before him with both hands, hard into the pit of Wentworth's stomach!

WENTWORTH ROLLED with the blow like a prizefighter, felt pain sear across his body at the muffled blast of the automatic. His right fist, looping low, caught the gunman on the side of the throat. The man jerked violently; the convulsion of his nerves stiffened him to his feet and held him erect through two dragging heartbeats. Then he slumped to the floor.

Wentworth took a slow step backward, took another. His shoulders were against the wall of the corridor outside Matthews' office. The burning in his side… his hand pressed to it absently. There was a ringing in his head. His ears popped. All at once, he could hear! The concussion of those close blasts had accomplished it. He could hear… and his head whipped toward the door of the apartment! The heavy crash of steel ringing on steel echoed through the corridor, and the loud shouts of men!

"Up! To the roof!" a man's crisp voice ordered. "Drop to the terrace!"

Wentworth pushed away from the wall. The silken rope… He snatched it up. But there would be no time. Those shouts were the police, and he recognized the crisp command of their chief. That was Stanley Kirkpatrick, the commissioner, at once the closest friend of Richard Wentworth and the Spider's fiercest enemy! And in his hand, on his person, was the sure proof that he was the Spider!

Wentworth's face turned grim, and his hand slapped to his vest pocket, as he stooped over the man he had killed with a powerful blow of his fist upon a certain nerve trunk. When he bounded up the corridor again, the dead man lay upon his back, and on the paling flesh of his forehead, there glowed the mocking, crimson seal of the Spider!

He whipped into the drawing room where the shattered corpses of Matthews' bodyguards lay in a grisly heap.

Not fifteen seconds later, a policeman darted out through the same doorway Wentworth had entered. There was a gun in his fist, and his face was set grimly. Another crowded behind him.

"Stay here," the first man rasped. "I'll get the door open!"

He reached the front entrance in a jump.

"Hold up, Commissioner!" he shouted. "I'll open the door!"

A few swift manipulations of the bolts, and the door flung wide. The first man through, gun in fist, was a lean, meticulously dressed man with a soldierly bearing. His blue eyes flashed frostily over the corridor, and his voice rang in command as he bounded toward the body upon the floor, toward Matthews' office. It was Commissioner Stanley Kirkpatrick, and it was not unusual that he should be the first to face whatever danger threatened his men. It was one reason why the entire force was slavishly devoted to him.

When the last of the police, in uniform and plain clothes, had stepped through that doorway and scattered to search and guard every corner of the penthouse, one man entered alone and casually. He was a small man, dapper in the extreme. His neat shoes were fantastically pointed, and the fitted fashionableness of his skirted coat, the high angle of the Homburg hat upon his head, marked him instantly for a Frenchman, though his face lacked the usual Gallic expressiveness. In fact, it showed nothing at all. HE STROLLED down the corridor behind the others and paused to stare down at the corpse of the gunman. He saw the seal, and still his face showed nothing….

"*Hola*, Kirkpatrick!" he said. "I have made the discovery! My quarry is not far from here, perhaps!"

Kirkpatrick appeared in the lighted oblong of Matthews' office, and his eyes followed the Frenchman's gloved hand.

"What is it, Chartres?" he asked, and impatience rasped beneath his polite manner.

The Frenchman shrugged, "Your *bête noir, M'sieur* Kirkpatrick," he murmured.

"The bane of your existence. I mean, in effect, the Spider! He has been here, but recently! This man has scarcely ceased to breathe!"

Kirkpatrick suppressed a sharp oath and reached the side of the man called Chartres in a single long stride. He glared down at the Spider's seal, whose crimson brilliance seemed to gather all the light in that dim hallway. A dark-visaged man in sergeant's uniform stepped to Kirkpatrick's elbow and received his sharp orders to make the search.

"Send word to the men surrounding the building, Sergeant Reams." Kirkpatrick's voice was low, sharp. "They are not to let even a man in uniform leave this building until I have personally released him. Understand?"

Sergeant Reams saluted, and there was grim purpose in his eyes as he strode away. Chartres was manipulating a dainty cigarette lighter. "He is bold, this Spider," he said casually. "He must have killed this man and imprinted the seal while we were outside the door. I do not think I should care to meet him unexpectedly."

Kirkpatrick's eyes were grimly sardonic. "It was for that you were appointed my deputy, Mr. Chartres," he said shortly. "You must not disappoint the mayor."

Chartres laughed lightly, and his face remained without expression. It was a disagreeable effect he produced. "I shall not come upon him unexpectedly, however," he said, "but according to my own plans. May I suggest that officers be sent at once to the home of this *M'sieur* Wentworth, who occasionally has been suspected? He has scarcely had time to arrive, and it would help if we could eliminate him from our list."

"Do as you wish," Kirkpatrick said shortly. "I have other matters at hand."

Sergeant Reams came striding down the hall. "Every room searched, sir," he reported. "He's not here. There are seven more dead men in the front room. Damnedest mess I ever saw. Looks like they all dived together in the middle of the room and cracked out their brains!"

Another policeman came out of the drawing room. His face was shaken, and his eyes staring. "No trace on the terrace, sir," he reported. "I looked for the Web, too."

Kirkpatrick nodded abruptly. His eyes were worried as he knuckled the spiked ends of his military mustache. "We'll look at these seven bodies of yours, Sergeant," he said. "Matthews' bodyguards, eh?"

29

Reams nodded and stood aside for Kirkpatrick. Chartres ambled after him and gazed without expression at the carnage. He dropped his cigarette, set a dapper foot upon it.

"Your pardon, *M'sieur* Kirkpatrick," he murmured. "Did the sergeant say seven corpses? Perhaps I am at fault, but I see only six!"

Reams swore, "There were seven! Damn it, a dead man can't get up and walk away!"

CHARTRES' LAUGHTER was light, cynical. "And did you ascertain that all seven were dead men, my sergeant, before the guard was withdrawn from the terrace? If you search it now, I think you will find... the Web, but no Spider—alas!"

Sergeant Reams swore and plunged toward the French doors opening on the terrace. Kirkpatrick was a stride behind him, but Sergeant Reams whirled to face him with a length of silken line in his hands. One end was knotted about a buttress in the terrace balustrade. The dark roof, two stories below, was empty of life. Not even the shadows moved as Kirkpatrick shouted commands. Police popped out of the roof hatch below a few moments later, but it was futile.

Once more the Spider had vanished from under the very eyes of the police!

Chartres' eyes were very bright. "Of a truth, *M'sieur* Kirkpatrick," he said softly, "the cleverness of this man has not been exaggerated. It is a contest of wits I shall enjoy! Will you order, now, this checkup at the home of *M'sieur* Wentworth?"

Kirkpatrick's eyes held their spark of cold anger, but Chartres was lighting another of his thin, pungent cigarettes and, aside from the glisten of his eyes, his face showed nothing. Kirkpatrick opened his lips, but closed them again grimly without speaking to Chartres. He gave Sergeant Reams the order to send a radio car to Wentworth's home, then turned back to the inspection of the apartment.

It was a weary time later that he returned to his office at headquarters through the deserted downtown streets. It was drawing on toward midnight, and this had been a fatiguing day. It was difficult to conceal his annoyance over Raoul Chartres' appointment over his head. The man was a naturalized American who had built up quite a reputation as a shrewd operative. Kirkpatrick was under no illusions as to his purpose. If he succeeded in snaring the Spider, a task in which Kirkpatrick had failed despite years of effort, it would mean the finish of Kirkpatrick's career as police commissioner; and the end of a work which he loved. Raoul Chartres would become commissioner in his stead!

Chartres, smoking another of his interminable cigarettes, was gazing placidly ahead of him, hands neatly clasped over the head of his cane.

"Do you contend, *m'sieur,*" he murmured, "that this Spider is a pure altruist? I'll admit I find that a conception most difficult. In my experience, men risk death for few things. For money, for power; on rare occasions, perhaps, for *l'amour...* for love. Altruism? But never."

Kirkpatrick's lips drew in a downward arc. "Your native country is at war, Mr. Chartres," he said.

"But yes! Ah, poor France!"

"You have, perhaps, known of men to die for patriotism?"

31

THE SPIDER

Chartres' head turned stiffly, and there was a dull red creeping into his forehead. "Let me understand you fully, *M'sieur* Kirkpatrick," he said slowly. "You do not wish, I think, to impugn my honor, my patriotism?"

Kirkpatrick's expression did not change. "I am not accustomed to speak in riddles," he said dryly. "When I accuse a man, there will be no doubt of my meaning. I point a parallel. Men have died for love of country. Is it so strange, then, that one man should have a greater love, and risk his life, for… all humanity?"

CHARTRES TOSSED his cigarette from the window, went about lighting another. "It is a conception a little strange," he said quietly. "You will permit that I find it difficult to join a murderer and a thief in my mind with… patriotism? And I could wish that your policemen had found *M'sieur* Wentworth at his home. He is a gentleman I should prefer to meet presently without suspicion. One of the great swordsmen of our time. Great with the foils, but with the sabre! Even the great De Rochefort has acknowledged him his master!" Chartres kissed his fingers delicately.

Kirkpatrick made no answer, and the limousine slid to a halt before police headquarters. He strode energetically up the steps, Chartres following more leisurely, and Kirkpatrick waited impatiently for him before ascending to his office. His secretary was absent from the desk in the outer chamber, and Kirkpatrick strode forward, flung wide the door.

A tall, commanding figure turned from the broad windows. "I began to think you'd never come back, Kirk," he said easily. "I've been waiting for ages to present my alibi."

32

Kirkpatrick's lips curved in a reluctant smile. He stepped aside, gestured toward the man at the window.

"I think you two should meet," he said to Chartres. "Dick, my new deputy, Raoul Chartres, charged with the capture of the Spider. Chartres, this is… Richard Wentworth!"

Wentworth's perfectly tailored person showed no traces of the life-and-death struggle he had undergone, thanks to a hurried but effective toilet made in his limousine. He had rested in Kirkpatrick's office, which he had entered after a ruse to draw the secretary from the door. Thus the man could not say at what time, precisely, he had arrived. There was still a slow, throbbing ache through his skull, and his eyes felt weak and drawn, but aside from that he was in perfect condition. He bowed with a continental clicking of his heels.

"*M'sieur* Chartres," he said affably, "you have a task which I do not envy you. The Spider is formidable."

Chartres' smile was all in his eyes. "I have already made contact with the gentleman, almost," he said. "You have, I see, had a slight accident, *M'sieur* Wentworth."

Wentworth lifted his brows, feeling the sharp stab of the tension which, for him, could never end. "Accident?" he asked gently, carelessly.

"Your hairs, *m'sieur*, they are singed!"

Wentworth laughed, "My valet was careless!" he acknowledged. "You will understand, *M'sieur* Chartres. A man of a certain age… his hair grows thin! Singeing strengthens what remains."

Chartres' smile increased. "But of course!"

33

Kirkpatrick was watching the two men narrowly. He swung abruptly behind his desk and motioned the others to chairs. "Your alibi, Dick," he said shortly. "How does it happen you know one is required?"

Wentworth shrugged. "Always, when the Spider appears nowadays, you want an alibi. And the radio carried news of a shooting affray which involved the Spider near where this witness, Hackett, was murdered. I was at home, and as nearly as I can make out, was talking to Nita over the phone at approximately the time of the shooting. But, Kirk, I have some theories about this Hackett murder!"

"Pardon, *m'sieur,*" Chartres interrupted smoothly. "This *Ma'amselle* Nita—you will pardon the informality—she is your fiancée?"

WENTWORTH'S SMILE was slow. "Ah, there I recognize the *Surete! Cherches la femme!* You are right. Miss Nita van Sloan is my fiancée."

"We have other methods," Chartres said quietly, "of which you will presently learn!"

"I, *M'sieur* Chartres?" The challenge was unmistakable beneath Wentworth's suavity.

Chartres bowed. "Since I understand, sir, that you frequently accompany the commissioner in his work!"

"Ah," Wentworth replied, bowing in turn. "I am glad to understand you completely." His voice had a taunt which brought fire to the eyes of the Frenchman. Wentworth had lived in France enough to know perfectly the Gallic temperament. They would hold in contempt any man who allowed the slightest challenge to his honor. But each, in his way, had served warning upon the other, and Wentworth knew that a bitter battle lay ahead, and how dangerous that contest might prove to… the Spider! He knew that a shrewd brain lay behind that impassive face, those keen eyes. Abruptly, turning toward Kirkpatrick, Wentworth knew a sharp stab of suspicion. It was no more than that… but the face of the Brand had been also without expression! Still, this man had been with Kirkpatrick at the penthouse of Waxy Matthews….

"You must permit me to give you a card to my club," he murmured to Chartres. "I can recommend the cuisine—but perhaps you dined there tonight with Kirk?"

Chartres' eyes grew sharp, grew challenging. "You seek… my alibi?" he asked, silkily. "I do not think I understand your thought, *m'sieur!*"

Wentworth's smile was cold, was without mirth. "I am only solicitous for your enjoyment, *M'sieur* Chartres, since undoubtedly you will remain with us for a long time. Many men have hunted the Spider, through many years. They were not, of course, trained in the *Sureté!*"

Chartres bowed, and suspicion still lurked beneath the surface candor of his gaze, but Wentworth had turned wholly to Kirkpatrick. "I have some theories of these killings, from the report on the air, Kirk," he said. "Also, I took the liberty of looking at some of the reports on your desk. I am quite sure that Hackett was murdered by an implosion!"

Kirkpatrick picked up a sheaf of papers on his desk, glanced at them quickly. Chartres leaned calmly on the head of his cane. "I'm not sure I follow you, *m'sieur.*"

"An explosion," Wentworth said swiftly, "occurs whenever the pressure of gases at one point is greater than the surrounding pressure. Implosions are known beneath the surface of the sea: When a submarine descends to too great a depth; when the air of a diver, at considerable depth, is suddenly released. Such implosive force can crush steel, can drive a man's entire body into the area of least resistance, his helmet. You have an equivalent situation when a man, accustomed to withstand a normal pressure of approximately fifteen pounds to the square inch, is thrust into a vacuum. He would explode, as do certain fish when brought up from the depths."

Kirkpatrick said sharply. "You mean, Dick, that a vacuum was produced close to Hackett's head, and that his skull... exploded to meet it? By the heavens, Dick, I believe you have something there! You couldn't know about it, of course, but at Matthews' apartment, there was even more proof of just such action. The door of the safe was *pulled* off. Creation of a powerful vacuum against its face would accomplish that. Six men were heaped together in the middle of the room, and their bodies had, to an extent, exploded! But, in God's name, how can we protect people against such a weapon?"

CHARTRES STRUCK his palms together softly. "Your deductive powers are truly remarkable, *M'sieur* Wentworth!" he cried. "We who saw all these deaths did not arrive at such a logical solution, but you who only hear and read of these things... you can fathom them! My compliments, *m'sieur!*"

Wentworth felt tension again. The Frenchman's suspicions were fully aroused, and with the realistic logic that was the particular trait of the intelligent Frenchman, he had at once seen the discrepancy! The man was already proving dangerous!

But Wentworth only arose to bow his acknowledgment. "You yourself, I am certain," he said, "would have arrived at the same conclusion. It was only that the horrors you witnessed distorted your perspective; while I, at a distance from the actual scene, was not thusly affected."

Chartres' eyes were bright with amusement. "I can see that the element of distance would be a distinct advantage in your case," he murmured.

Wentworth laughed in genuine enjoyment. If the man's brain was as sharp as his tongue, this would be a battle worth fighting! He always enjoyed a good opponent, and he found himself warming in anticipation of his next encounter with this chap. If only the threat that hung over the people he loved and served were not so horrible!

"I am going to put a little distance between myself and these headquarters now, if it is permitted," Wentworth said. "In fact, I need a bit of sleep. But I wanted you to know these things, Kirk."

Kirkpatrick rose, and his eyes flashed hostility toward Chartres. He would be swifter in his duty than any man alive if he could prove Wentworth guilty. He would not have swerved from the conviction of his own brother, had conviction been just. It was this mutual integrity of spirit, and the admiration the two held for each other, that had helped to draw Kirkpatrick and Wentworth into very close friendship.

"There is no reason to detain you, Dick," Kirkpatrick said steadily.

Wentworth nodded easily to Kirk, clicked his heels at Chartres. "We shall, no doubt, meet again, *M'sieur* Chartres," he said. "I would like to witness your first meeting with the Spider. And I have no doubt that he will welcome the contest. He is a notable strategist, and a fighter!"

"I am complimented," Chartres said, and there was sincerity in his voice.

Wentworth nodded and strode from the office, and the two men left behind stared at the closed door. Kirkpatrick knew a breath of regret, which his conscience instantly challenged. He was afraid that Chartres would prove too much for the Spider. He was afraid of what the Spider's capture would reveal… His lips tightened. He had warned Dick Wentworth! No living man could forever avoid his destiny, his downfall.

Chartres was smoothing on his pale lemon kid gloves, and there was thoughtfulness in his eyes. *Ma foi!* This thing would not be so simple as he had thought! This Wentworth seemed a man of honor, *un gentilhomme veritable.* Difficult to think of him as a murderer, but men will do many things for power, for ambition. Himself, for instance… Chartres closed his thoughts. Kirkpatrick was speaking.

"I wonder when this killer will strike again," he said heavily. "He is damnably clever!"

Chartres' eyes were on the door. He said softly, "I think he will strike very soon!"

Kirkpatrick's voice rapped out in challenge. "I referred to this Brand, Chartres!"

Chartres was lighting a cigarette. He looked at Kirkpatrick, and the reflection of the fire flickered in his dark, clever eyes. "But yes, of course!" he said. "That is your task. My own... is to take this Spider! If you will excuse me, I shall begin mine!"

He followed Wentworth from the building.

CHAPTER 3
PAY FOR A KILLER

THOUGH IT had been fear, rather than prescience, which dictated their predictions, both Kirkpatrick and Chartres were right! The Spider and the Brand—both would strike again before the dawn!

Outside headquarters, Wentworth climbed carelessly into the limousine that Jackson slid to the curb. The instant they were underway, he spoke.

"I shall be followed," he said, "but give no sign that you realize it, and do not attempt to lose the gentleman. That should give us a good lead and presently, when you turn a dark corner, we will change places! Fortunately, you wear dark trousers and shoes. I will drive the car to the garage in your tunic and cap; you will go to the apartment, get on a spare tunic and... wait!"

Jackson was already unfastening his tunic as the car turned the first corner, but his voice was heavy with regret. "You're going into action, Major, and without me."

Wentworth smiled, and his eyes were gentle. Such loyalty was given so few men! "I must, Jackson," he said quietly. "You will be needed at the house. Ram Singh will take all incoming calls, and refuse information on the pretext that he cannot be sure of the caller's identity. If Kirkpatrick, or a man with a slight French accent calls, you will put a warning message on our shortwave radio at once."

"Code, sir?"

Wentworth's eyes crinkled with amusement. "Imitate a police broadcast, Jackson," he said. "You will say, 'Deputy Frenchy Chartrez'—pronounce it *Charrtres*—'call headquarters at once!'"

"Never heard of the man in my life," Jackson said.

"But you will!" Wentworth told him grimly. "I think if you turn the next corner, we will have time for our changeover. Deputy Chartres is about two blocks behind us!"

THE MAN whom Wentworth called the Brand was five blocks ahead of him. He was driving placidly up Fifth Avenue into the thickening after-theatre traffic. On the seat beside him the red robe was neatly folded, and there were other bulky objects within it. Against the cushion leaned a short, thick cane... and the Brand's lips were thinly smiling. Unconsciously, he was whistling between his teeth an old-fashioned hymn.

Matters had been comparatively simple so far. True, he had probably lost one of his three hireling gunmen, but he was easily replaced. It had been very shrewd of him to send the deaf-and-dumb man to kill the Spider. Then, if the encroaching police captured him in the apartment of Waxy Matthews, they could learn nothing!

The take for the night was well over fifty thousand dollars.

Chicken feed, of course, but not bad for a beginning. Not bad. And the Bolt—as he called the deadly device he had perfected—was an excellent weapon, even better than he had hoped. A chuckle burst from the man's slitted mouth. Their heads looked so funny after the Bolt spoke! Well, he would have a chance to laugh again very shortly....

A touch of worry clouded his shallow eyes for an instant. He could not be sure that the Spider was dead, of course. It was incredible that the Bolt should have spoken to the Spider in its sweet voice of thunder—and that afterward, the Spider should be able to rise and charge! Something like a chill touched the spine of the Brand at the memory. Criminals had felt that faint brush of fear before this, at thought of the Spider! There was a slight doubt in the Brand's mind. Damn it, was the man *human?*

The Brand shrugged the thought aside. That was nonsense. He alone was more than human, as he would prove this night. His eyes swung affectionately toward the short, thick cane. He whipped the car to the left, toward Times Square. There were certain lawyers there who kept office hours even later than this, one Henry Small among them. Small was unimportant, of course, but he had double-crossed Big Jack Donnelly, a wealthy crook. Big Jack didn't know it yet, but he was going to pay well for Henry Small's removal!

The car swung to the curb, and the Brand got out. His eyes lifted to a lighted window, whose gold letters stood out blackly now:

HENRY SMALL—Attorney at Law.

The Brand smiled slowly. The cane swung in his hand. He whistled softly through his teeth… A moment with Henry Small, and then a swift visit to Big Jack Donnelly. Big Jack's safe was always well lined, and the Brand thought he could persuade him to open it! If not… The Brand took the cane in both hands. His palm ran along it affectionately, and then once more the Brand frowned.

If the Spider got in his way, then… God help the Spider! He would not escape again!

When the muted thunder roll that was the voice of the Bolt sounded, no one in the street noticed it. The subterranean rumble of subways, the clatter of trolley cars, was loud. And no one noticed that the sign—

HENRY SMALL—Attorney at Law.

—no longer showed against the lighted oblong of the office window.

After that single first rumble, moments of silence ticked past. Afterward, there was a sound that no one could ignore! It was the thunderclap of ten electric storms rolled into one!

A coasting radio patrol car halted suddenly in the street, and a uniformed man popped out on the running board, his throat tight as he stared upward. High up in the building wall, there was a gaping hole that showed the gaunt steel framework!

"An explosion!" the cop rasped. "Park it, and let's go! Phone headquarters! Ambulances, wrecking squad!"

He hit the pavement running, and the police car wedged into

the curb. It was just ahead of a small coupé on whose seat rested a red bundle, but the attention of the two officers was on the building itself. A crowd was already gathering. Men and women stared upward, pointing. A traffic cop was pinwheeling his arms to speed the stream of autos past the spot, and up Broadway a mounted officer galloped.

THAT WAS the way matters stood when a man sauntered unhurriedly from the entrance of the building, carelessly swinging a short, thick cane. The pleased smile on his lips tautened a little as he saw the two policemen running toward him, but that was all.

"Wait!" the first cop yelled at him. "Wait a minute, there! Nobody leaves this building!"

The smile on the man's lips grew thinner. "Were you speaking to me?" he asked, and the cane was horizontal in his right hand.

"Yeah, you!"

The smile vanished, and the lips twisted into a snarl. His hands closed tightly on the cane, and blue-white light flickered from its end. Through the air slashed a streak like a controlled electric spark, and it snapped between the two policemen. Once more, the soft thunderous rumble of the Bolt smote the night air! The two policemen did a curious thing. They pivoted like grotesque dancers in mid-stride. They whipped together, headfirst, as if in that split-second they had deliberately decided to knock their heads together! The violence of that simultaneous inward leap whipped their feet off the earth, snapped their arms wide and loose, like those of articulated dolls. Their caps flew into the air. Their heads... broke open.

Then they lay quivering, in a heap upon the pavement. The Brand stood motionless. His lips parted and the laughter that came from them was thin, icy.

No one in the crowd laughed. Most of them were in flight, screaming, shouting their hoarse terror. A man slammed against a light post, and the blood spurted from his nostrils. His feet jerked as he hit the pavement flat on his back. His limbs quivered, jerked. And a scream bubbled in his throat.

On the pavement behind the policemen were a few who had not fled. They were a tumbled heap there on the cold pavement, the cold white pavement that was slowly turning red.

The man with the short thick cane pivoted slowly, and twice more he squeezed the innocuous-seeming stick. The traffic policeman leaped backward and spread himself against the front of an automobile. The windshield of that car spread forward over the street, and the driver plunged forward across his wheel and lay there, limply, upon the hood. Up the street, the galloping horse jerked up its head in an incredible arc that smashed against the face of the mountie upon its back. Its forefoot lifted straight up from the pavement, and then man and steed pitched to the street.

The Brand stood and laughed a little. He was still laughing, with a dry and horrible emphasis, when he climbed into his coupé and jockeyed it out from the curb. The street was quite empty when he drove eastward again, empty of the living… Above the hum of his engine could be heard a faint, shrill whistling, an old, old hymn….

The whistling broke off, and the Brand chuckled. "Next stop, my friend, will be the office of Big Jack Donnelly," he said. He reached out and patted the cane that was as short and thick as the death-stiffened corpse of a viper.

"My friend…" he whispered.

BIG JACK DONNELLY'S office was headquarters of a powerful union which always won its strikes. That is, the union won. The men who were its members did not. Not many unions were like that, but sometimes the crooks moved in on them. Hard to prove they were crooks; certain death for a member to try… when the boss was a man as smart and dangerous as Big Jack Donnelly.

The union was a source of income, but it was small-time stuff for Donnelly. His gambling rackets paid a bigger graft, but those were secret, more or less. They were what had earned him his sobriquet in the underworld: Big Jack. Nothing small-time about him. When he went into a game it was big jack or nothing….

Big Jack Donnelly didn't take a great many precautions against hijackers or police raids. Didn't have to. Of course, there were always a half dozen "union officers" around headquarters, and of course they had guns… with permits. But Big Jack's was a little quieter than usual tonight. The men in the inner office were ill-at-ease, restless. They didn't even play cards; they sat stiffly at attention. Their hands kept straying to their guns, and their eyes turned time and again toward the door of that inner, soundproofed office.

Just above that door was a red bulb like an exit light. When Big Jack wanted them, that light would flash on. Time enough

to pull their guns, then, and go crashing in. The man nearest the door took out a key and looked at it.

Big Jack must be a little scared tonight. First time he'd ever given anybody a key to his office, even for a half-hour, even to Louis Frank. Yeah, a little scared. But hell, you couldn't blame him. Look what had happened to big-time Waxy Matthews! And that double-crossing mouthpiece, Hank Small! Yeah....

Louis Frank slipped the key back into his vest pocket, and the lights in the outer office went out.

Two policemen whipped together
head first... as the crowd fled.

Frank jumped to his feet. "Hey! Who's getting funny!" he snapped, and his voice was suddenly hoarse. "Turn them lights on! Turn them on, I say, for Chr—"

His voice was cut off with the suddenness of a disconnected radio. Men were scrambling to their feet. A chair crashed to the floor. It was, perhaps, two minutes before the lights flicked on again.

Louis Frank sat slumped in his chair beside the door, and the door was closed. The red light wasn't burning. Louis Frank shook his head, rubbed the side of his neck, and lifted to his feet.

"Hey, what happened!" he snapped. "Who turned off them lights?!"

Nobody answered him, and Louis Frank pawed for his vest pocket and pulled out the key. "He said we wasn't to bother him until he showed that light," he muttered. After all, the lights had just burned off and on. His throat—well, he *thought* something had jabbed him there. But he still had the key, didn't he? And Big Jack didn't like his orders disobeyed. Still, it was pretty funny. Lights going on and off. Power failure, maybe. Louis Frank sat stiffly down in the chair and touched his gun again. The other men sat down more tensely than before. Pretty funny. Yeah....

INSIDE BIG JACK'S office, things were pretty funny, too. But the man behind the desk didn't seem to think so. He was staring, with wide-strained eyes, toward the door, and that was where the man who was laughing stood. The laughter was thin and ugly, and it came from a face that had utterly no expression at all, and a gleaming bald head. The man seemed to have no arms; he was covered from shoulders to floor in a long red robe. Little flickers of blue-white light played about him! The Brand!

"I've come for my pay, Big Jack Donnelly," said the Brand. "My pay for… removing Henry Small, attorney-at-law!"

The man behind the desk touched his tongue to his lips. His face was twisted with fright, but somehow it didn't show in his blue-gray eyes. They were very steady, very calm, those eyes.

"Who—who are you?" he asked hoarsely. "What do you want?"

The figure in the red robe moved forward with an effect of gliding. "You may call me the Brand!" his voice whispered. "I've told you why I come here, Big Jack Donnelly! Did you think you could keep me away with that fool guard of yours in the outer office? I walked through them. I took the key from your guard, and put it back in his pocket, and they didn't even see me! No man can stop the Brand!"

The man behind the desk touched his tongue to his lips again. Behind him was a strong light. It was focused full upon the Brand, so that the Brand could not see the facial details of his intended victim.

"Let me get this straight," said the man behind the desk, and his voice was very clear and precise, almost like a man who spoke into a microphone and wanted to be sure he was understood. "You come to the office of Big Jack Donnelly to be paid for killing Henry Small, attorney-at-law. You call yourself the Brand. What kind of racket is this, anyhow?"

"You'll pay, Big Jack!" said the Brand.

"I haven't said I wouldn't, have I?" There was a whine in Big

Jack's voice that did not match with the steadiness of his eyes. "I just want to know. God, you're a smart guy, to figure out a new racket like this! And you bumped off Waxy Matthews and six of his men? One guy, all alone?"

"One man, all alone." The Brand's voice was exultant. "Just one friend and I! The fee is a hundred grand, Big Jack. Payable right now. Or do you want a receipt put in your hand *afterward?*"

"God, no!" the other man cried hoarsely. "I just want to understand. You go around and kill guys that need killing, and then collect from the big shot that wants the guy out of the way, is that it? And if they don't pay, you rub them out, too! That takes guts."

The Brand said flatly, "You've talked enough! Open the safe!"

The man stumbled to his feet. "I just wanted to know your racket. Look, how do I know you won't bump me off when I open the safe, huh? How do I know that? Maybe Waxy Matthews opened his safe, and you bumped him off afterward!"

"Maybe I did," the Brand whispered. "Does it matter? But I might want you to live for a while, Big Jack. I might want you to work for me. Every crook in the city is going to work for me before long. Those that don't… will meet—*my friend The Bolt!*

THE MAN behind the desk was standing now. His voice changed. "That's the whole story," he said quietly. "You've heard the Brand, you men of the Underworld, and you've heard his plot. If I don't kill him in the next few minutes, you'll know what to do to him!"

The Brand leaped forward. Something under his robe, like the end of a cane, ground hard into the side of the speaker.

"What the hell are you talking about?" he snapped.

The man smiled, and he looked much less like Big Jack Donnelly. His voice was quiet, grave. "Turn on the radio in the corner behind you," he said.

The Brand jammed the point of the cane harder against the man's ribs. There was a blazing fury in his shallow eyes, but the gaze that met his was steady, unwavering… and unafraid! The Brand backed off slowly, turned on the radio. The man he confronted spoke quietly, and his voice curiously came from two places at once: it came from his lips, and from the radio receiver beside the Brand!

"Really very simple," said the voice. "Every big shot in the city has heard your voice and your racket. So have the police. They were called up in advance and warned to listen for this broadcast. A very simple device, don't you think, and one that…."

While he still spoke, the door behind the Brand fanned wide and the six henchmen of Big Jack Donnelly slammed into the room. Their guns were in their fists, and as they stood there in the entrance, the red light of the signal above their heads spilled down across their white faces.

"Kill him!" the radio bellowed.

At the same instant, the man who had spoken hurled himself flat on the floor behind the desk. As he fell, two heavy black automatics leaped into his fists and, as they began to speak, a flat, mocking laughter poured from his lips… the laughter *of the Spider!*

His first shot blasted across the office, and its voice was drowned out in a ripping peal of thunder! A blue-white flare lit the room and the Spider—for it was he, disguised as Big Jack Donnelly—felt the slashing pain of it across his eardrums. The pull of the implosion released by the Brand fluttered his clothing, tugged at his hair. He flung himself to his feet, crouched, ominous with those two black guns in his fists! There was no fear, no dread in his strong-lined face, only the passionless fury of the Spider facing a vulture of the Underworld. His guns were ready... but they did not speak!

The Brand had vanished!

Where the six men had crouched in the doorway, there was a welter of human bodies. From behind the desk Wentworth seized the rest of the Spider's garb, hastily donned it, and surveyed the room. As he stared, two of the men struggled to their feet. Their faces were haggard. There was blood on their mouths. They stared at the crouching Spider through a long still moment, then their eyes wavered. Wentworth's eyes flicked where they looked. The blast had wrenched open the door of the closet where he had stuffed Big Jack Donnelly after binding and gagging him. There was a placard pinned to Big Jack's coat.

"Take warning from this," it read, "and give up your control of the union. This might just as easily have been placed on your forehead. Next time...."

Below was affixed... *the seal of the Spider!*

Wentworth swore softly, bounded forward across the room, and in the same instant the two men snapped out of their paralysis. They alone had survived the fearful shock of that discharged implosion, and Wentworth guessed that the Brand had dared not release his full power lest he kill himself also. That thought was flicking through his mind as he leaped across the room, and he saw that realization had penetrated the numbed brains of the two gunmen at the same time. Their guns came up… aimed straight at the Spider!

IN ONE more bound, Wentworth reached these men. As their guns spoke, the Spider's automatics whipped down. There was the clash of metal meeting metal, and the guns were driven from their hands. The Spider struck once more, and the two men slumped to the floor, knocked cold. They were crooks, yes, but not killers, to his knowledge. When the Spider killed, it was because the victims deserved to die for their crimes!

Wentworth bounded past the huddle of the slain, toward the doorway through which he knew the Brand must have leaped no more than thirty seconds before. The dark exit to the hallway loomed ahead, and beyond that was a thin blue flicker of light. Wentworth laughed softly as he hurled himself toward it. The Brand still waited! This time, the Brand wanted to make sure of the Spider! Well, it was mutual! The swift guns of the Spider would challenge this strange man-made lightning!

Wentworth leaped forward, and behind him he heard the radio rasp into life again. "Calling Deputy Frenchy Chartrez," said the voice. "Call your headquarters at once! Calling Deputy Frenchy Chartrez, call your headquarters at once! *Urgent!*"

Wentworth heard the sharp emphasis on that last word of the code message uttered by Jackson. Not only had Kirkpatrick or Chartres called his home then, but they were on the way there! No other meaning could conceivably be applied to that 'urgent'! The Spider's disguised lips drew thinly together, but he did not check his forward leap. The Spider was in the midst of battle against an enemy of mankind, and no personal consideration could turn him aside!

Just within the doorway, Wentworth stopped. He thrust out his gun and fanned death through that hallway. The flicker of light increased sharply. His hand felt the scorching heat, and the gun leaped from his fist. An oath jerked on Wentworth's lips. He straightened, glanced at his remaining automatic—and plunged into the hallway!

He saw the Brand, a brilliant figure in red, silhouetted against the blue-white flicker of the light that played about him. And the gun jarred in the Spider's fist, jarred and jarred again. He filled the hallway with the old familiar thunder of his own forty-five-caliber gun. The figure in red leaped backward, but it was doubled over like a broken doll. Wentworth's laughter sprang sharply from his lips. It was the quarter-ton impact of his lead that was driving the Brand to his death.

He laughed, and once more thunder rolled along that narrow hallway! Echoed and re-echoed!

Wentworth's laughter was plucked from his lips. He felt his whole body lift, then fall to the floor. His senses wavered. The bolt had missed, had been the last dying flutter of the Brand. It had sped toward the ceiling, but Wentworth's limbs refused his orders.

Dimly, he heard the radio repeating the call for "Frenchy Chartrez!" It must be damnably urgent for Jackson to repeat like that. The police… why, damn it, the police would be on their way here, too! That radio broadcast of his would have brought them. No need for them to trace down the beam, when he had told them where he was. Yes, the police were on the way here, and speeding toward his home was that clever nemesis of the Spider, Raoul Chartres.

Wentworth tried to drive himself to his feet, but his legs were rubber; his hands had no feeling. Somewhere, a siren began to sing what well might be the death-dirge of the Spider!

CHAPTER 4
HALFWAY TO DEATH

LABORIOUSLY, WENTWORTH rose from the floor; by a severe concentration of will, he grasped his automatics. He stumbled down the hallway toward where the man in the red robe had fallen. Despite the pressure of danger, Wentworth felt exultation. He had stopped the Brand before he could fairly organize his campaign of terror and murder… he hoped.

Anxiety stabbed him, and he sent the beam of a special pocket flashlight along the floor. The figure in the red robe was still sprawled there. His fall had knocked off a mask of steel shaped like an impassive face, a mask that cupped, too, the top of the skull so that the man seemed to have a bald and gleaming head. The face revealed was ruthless, and Wentworth's lips were grim as he bent to press the seal of the Spider on the low forehead below the bristling red hair. Wentworth frowned; this was the face of a murderer beyond a doubt, but scarcely a clever man. This man was merely a stooge.

55

A rasping curse cut short Wentworth's search for the weird weapon. He whipped about. There, where the light from the outer office spilled across the hallway, crouched the two men he had knocked out. Guns were in their fists, but they were still uncertain of their feet.

"The Spider," rasped Louis Frank. "I tell you it's the Spider! The Chief is in there, with that sign on his chest! Burn him down, you fool!"

The men lifted their guns, and Wentworth hurled his still blazing flashlight squarely at their faces. In the streets, the shriek of sirens was suddenly loud, and Wentworth muttered an oath as he leaped toward his two attackers. Instinctively, they dodged the hurtling torch. Its beam struck across their eyes. And such was the furious speed of Wentworth's forward leap that he was upon them before they had time to recover. His fists drove the men away from the door.

Then he was across the outer office, had popped in through the door of Big Jack's inner sanctum. His gun was in his fist, and his mind was racing furiously. There was a chance that he could escape by the window and the silken Web from the roof, as he had entered. But it would be slow, painfully slow, and might not succeed. He could not afford the delay… or Chartres would reach his home ahead of him!

Wentworth's lips tightened grimly as he recognized the thing that he must do. He must fool those men in the hallway, get past the police at the front door… and steal a police car! It was the only way he could reach home in time!

As he propped open the soundproofed door of Big Jack's

office, he heard the crash of police axes biting into the thick outer doors of the building, which was a converted warehouse. Wentworth began shooting.

He sent his bullets carefully into the ceiling as he leaped toward the spot where Big Jack Donnelly still lay unconscious on the floor. The Spider shouted hoarsely, as if in an agony of pain.

"Don't!" he shouted. "Don't shoot again, Big Jack!"

He was bending over Big Jack now, jerking the sign off his coat, and pinning it on his own, slashing the ropes that bound his wrists. He laughed, and it was the hoarse bellow of Big Jack's deep voice that sounded through the room!

"So you don't like it, Spider?" he rasped.

Twice more he fired the heavy automatic, then he leaped across the room toward the door into the outer office. The fragments of the slashed rope dangled from his gun wrist, the sign bearing the Spider seal was on his chest. He staggered out where the two crooks stood with dangling guns in their fists.

"You cheap punks!" Wentworth snarled in imitation of Big Jack's voice. "You quit on me when I need you, hunh? I got a good mind to burn your guts!"

THE BIG gun in his fist snouted toward the two, and there was an ugly twist to his disguised lips. "You leave Big Jack to fight the Spider alone, hunh?"

Louis Frank whined, "Cheez, Big Jack, he knocked us cuckoo, and—"

"Never mind," Big Jack snapped. "I killed him! I did it, single-handed! That's the kind of guy I am!"

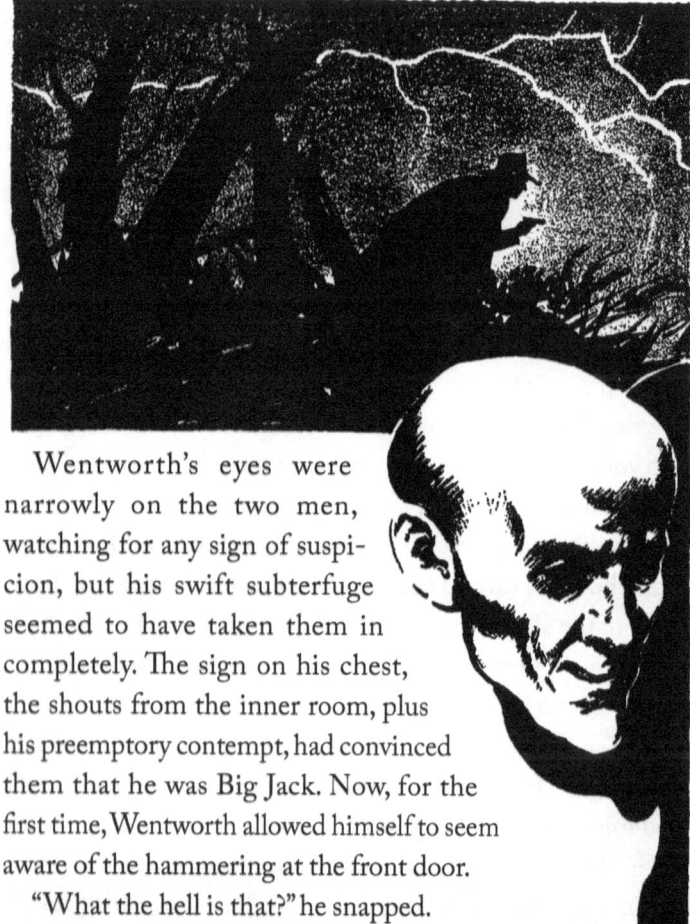

Wentworth's eyes were narrowly on the two men, watching for any sign of suspicion, but his swift subterfuge seemed to have taken them in completely. The sign on his chest, the shouts from the inner room, plus his preemptory contempt, had convinced them that he was Big Jack. Now, for the first time, Wentworth allowed himself to seem aware of the hammering at the front door.

"What the hell is that?" he snapped.

"The cops!" Louis Frank stammered, cringingly. "I guess the Spider called them in. He was broadcasting a talk with this guy in red, and the Spider killed him, too! He's down the hall!"

Wentworth stood for a moment, frowning. "All right," he

CHATRES

DONNELLY

BOSHER

The gaunt silhouettes of the winter-stripped trees were like the bars of a giant prison window. Through them, Wentworth wove a swift way. He heard the beat of running feet... behind him...

snapped. "I'll let them in! You two mugs lie down on the floor like you're still knocked out. I killed the Spider, without your help, and I'm damned if I'll let you suck in on the credit, understand? Don't even poke your sniveling noses in my office!"

He thrust past them and went

rapidly down the hallway, clattered down the steps toward the front door. He saw the bright edge of an axe bite through the wooden panel as he ran toward it.

"Wait!" he yelled hoarsely. "Wait, out there! I'll open the door! I'd of come sooner, but the Spider…" He fumbled open the bolts, and when the doors swung wide, he clapped a hand to his belly and went forward heavily, reeling, as if he had a bullet through his abdomen. "I got the Spider," he whispered hoarsely. "In my office… for God's sake, get me to a doctor, quick!"

Beneath the down-hanging hair of his wig, Wentworth saw Kirkpatrick striding forward, but Chartres was nowhere in sight. He wouldn't be, damn him! He would be on the way to Wentworth's home!

Still the uniformed police hesitated, guns ready in their fists. Wentworth stood still, legs braced, bent far forward over his clutching hands. He swayed for a moment, slipped to his knees.

"For God's sake," he whispered.

Kirkpatrick's voice rang out crisply, "Get him to the ambulance, there! Sergeant Reams, with me! If he's got the Spider… Cassidy, guard Donnelly! Stay with him at the hospital!"

Two men had their hands under Wentworth's arms now and were helping him toward an ambulance halfway up the block. An intern in a white coat came loping lazily toward them.

"Put him down," the intern called.

"Go to hell!" Wentworth snarled. "No damned amateur is going to probe in my guts! Get me in that ambulance and call Doc Parsiddy. Tell him Big Jack Donnelly says get to the hospital and get there fast, or else!"

The intern hesitated, shrugged his shoulders; and the police carried Wentworth on toward the ambulance. They heaved him into the back. The cop called Cassidy scrambled in afterward, and the intern jumped up on the step.

"Hospital, Mike!" he called. "Emergency case!" He peered toward Wentworth with a crooked, thin-lipped smile. "Probably D.O.A.," he added with a shrug.

"Don't say that, doc!" Wentworth pleaded, with sudden fright in his voice as the ambulance surged forward. "Hey, look at this hole, Doc, and see if you can plug it!"

THE INTERN stood easily in the swaying ambulance, bent toward Wentworth. It was the moment Wentworth had planned for. His fist arched up, and he rolled his body to get all possible weight behind the blow. The intern's head was driven upward and he pitched backward across the policeman. He swore in a thin, strained voice, and Wentworth was instantly on his feet. His fists swung, and the rocking of his broad shoulders told of their force. One-two, one-two. Intern and policeman were sprawled out, unconscious, on the floor. In a single long leap, Wentworth reached the forward end of the ambulance. He poked out the glass with the muzzle of his automatic and thrust the cold nose against the driver's ear.

"Straight eastward," he ordered coldly. "Keep that siren going and smash the traffic wide open!"

They had sped six blocks before Wentworth became aware of the persistent blasting of an automobile horn behind them. He twisted his head about, and relief swelled in his chest. It was one of his own camouflaged coupés; a powerful motor was under that battered hood! There was a girl's lovely face behind the wheel. Her smile, strangely soft in that moment of tension, moved Wentworth. She was Nita van Sloan, his fiancée. She had been nearby all the time, operating the shortwave radio relay from the coupé so that Wentworth could broadcast the evidence he had drawn from the Brand. He had summoned Nita by telephone as soon as he found out, by police radio, that Henry Small had been murdered.

Wentworth turned back to the driver, "North at the next corner," he snarled. "Then stop!"

The driver whipped the ambulance over in a whining skid, slammed on brakes… and Wentworth jabbed stiffened fingers into a nerve center in the side of the man's throat. The man slumped forward, unconscious, across the wheel. Wentworth was instantly out of the ambulance and loping toward the coupé. It scarcely hesitated as the door flung wide, then snapped forward again… toward his home!

Wentworth settled into the seat, and his fingers were instantly at work stripping off the disguise of Big Jack Donnelly. He threw the fragments of it out the window as the car tore along under Nita's skillful hands.

"You got Jackson's warning?" she asked quickly. "Chartres is on the way there!"

Wentworth nodded, and there was a smile on his lips as he glanced toward Nita's intent, chiseled profile. The chestnut curls were whipped gloriously back beneath the close brim of her felt hat. Her rounded chin was set firmly… but nothing could change the soft sweetness of her mouth. Not even the fear she felt for the man she loved.

"I thought, dear, that I told you to go straight home as soon as the broadcast was finished!" he said. "You were in terrible danger in the neighborhood of a battle between the Brand and Donnelly—or me!"

Nita's eyes flashed toward him for a single instant, and their violet depths were warm with her love, though her lips mocked him with a smile.

"Next time," she jibed, "I'll do what you tell me—and then I'll come down and jeer at you behind the bars of Stanley Kirkpatrick's jail! I never saw such a man, for getting into trouble!"

Wentworth smiled back at her. He was ripping off his coat, fishing out Jackson's discarded tunic and his uniform cap from behind the seat. "Lucky thing you're on my side," he said. "Even Kirkpatrick didn't see through the trick back there, but you did!"

Nita's eyes were straight forward, but the smile that curved her red lips was tender now. "I'd know you anywhere, anytime, Dick," she said. "If I were blind, I think I'd still know you!"

They were silent then, while the car roared southward toward Wentworth's home. Wentworth knew Nita's unspoken thought, that her love would always find him out when he needed her most, as time and again, in his fierce struggles with the beasts of the underworld jungles, he had found Nita in his time of greatest need. His hand rested for a moment, warmly, on her shoulder. It was terribly unfair to Nita, this life they led, but it could be no other way. God knew he had fought against his love for her, feeling his life already foresworn when they had met. It was prob-

63

able that they would never know the quiet happiness of their love; they must deny themselves, that others might have safe, happy homes and children. Nita's eyes met his, and she read his heart as always. Their moments together were so brief, so brief. **WENTWORTH JERKED** his head, flung aside the thoughts. "I think I killed the Brand there tonight," he said. "If I can beat Chartres home, if I left no clues behind, this battle may be at an end for the moment. I'm not sure. That dead man— he didn't seem to be clever enough. And the Brand was out of sight long enough to change disguise with one of his henchmen. Also, this man I killed bore a close resemblance to another who tried to kill me at Matthews' place."

Nita laughed. "Even if he's still alive, he's finished in the Underworld," she said. "I phoned a dozen of the big men of crookdom to make sure they would hear the broadcast. They'll be on the lookout for him now... What are your plans?"

Wentworth shook his head. "Too soon to say. Drop me at the door. Lord—if Chartres is already there...."

The coupé swung into Fifth Avenue, and Wentworth caught an oath on his lips. He was only a half-block from his home, but there was a police limousine speeding toward the same spot. He could identify it instantly from the red leer of its headlights, even if the siren were not moaning.

"Quickly!" he whispered. "Drop me at the side entrance... and get for home. If they follow you, lose them!"

Nita nodded, and an instant later, jammed on brakes. Wentworth stepped out with the jaunty, half-swaggering stride of Jackson.

"So long, toots!" he called. "Thanks for the lift… and I'll be seeing you!"

Nita's tone was imperceptibly changed. "So long, big boy!"

The coupé rolled, and Wentworth moved swiftly, but with a deceptive appearance of nonchalance, toward the door. He entered the apartment building as the big limousine rounded to the curb. His cautious backward glance brought a curse to his lips. Nita was deliberately swinging in a U-turn squarely into the path of the police car!

The limousine jerked to a halt within inches of the coupé, and Nita's face was at the window. Wentworth saw in a quick glance that she had whipped off her hat so that her hair was wild about her face. There was a smear of lipstick on her lips, and her cheeks showed over-rouged. It didn't seem possible that it was Nita, but she had learned the arts of disguise under a master—under the Spider himself!

"Sa-ay!" she bawled at the driver of the police car. "Why don't you look where you're going, you dumb flatfoot! Think you own the city streets? Gee, you cops give me a pain. Always talking about careful driving, and then hogging the streets!"

A quick smile crossed Wentworth's lips. Nita would get away with it, all right. She had a driving permit and registration under an assumed name which she could use at need….

The dapper figure of Raoul Chartres bounded out of the rear of the police car!

Wentworth stepped into the automatic private elevator that led to his apartment and pressed the button. He would have perhaps two minutes in his apartment, no more. He studied his face in the elevator mirror, seeking some traces of the makeup he had discarded, used his handkerchief to remove a final smear.

At the doorway of his apartment, he jabbed in the key. He heard quick footsteps, and Jackson was at the entrance.

"Chartres, on his way up!" Wentworth snapped. "Miss Nita dropped me. The old coupé stunt. She delayed the cops." He concocted a story to serve as an alibi—one which Jackson would be able to quote if quizzed alone.

Jackson's brow was furrowed as he took in the swift staccato of information. Wentworth's other comrade-at-arms, the turbaned Sikh, Ram Singh, snatched the tunic and cap as Wentworth discarded them, accepted the tie he ripped off, and imperturbably held out a dressing robe for him.

"Right," Jackson acknowledged. "Chartres, Kirkpatrick both phoned. Ram Singh refused to disturb you. Said you were worn out—had fallen asleep in your clothes."

"Good!" Wentworth replied, and an easy smile came to his lips. "Ram Singh, keep in the background, and listen for orders."

As he finished the sentence, the doorbell pealed.

JACKSON GRINNED. He waited a moment, then snapped aside the cover of the peephole in the center of the panel. To one side, Wentworth rumpled his hair, rubbed color into his cheeks, knuckled his eyes to give them the appearance of sleep. He rumpled his shirt with swift twisting hands.

"Yes, sir," Jackson was saying through the peephole. "If you're from the police I guess I'll have to. Ram Singh, call the master, and tell him a guy named Chartrez from police headquarters wants to see him. No sir, Mr. Chartrez, you'll have to wait until the boss says it's okay."

Wentworth waited through a long moment, then nodded to Jackson. He called, with an effect of distance. "It's all right, Jackson," he said, breaking the words with a yawn. "Ask Mr. Chartrez in."

Chartres appeared amiable, despite the anger that sparkled in his eyes. "You are faithfully served, *M'sieur* Wentworth!" he murmured. "I called you, twice, from headquarters and they refused to arouse you!"

Wentworth smoothed back his hair ruefully. "I'm sorry," he said slowly. "If Jackson had been here… When did you get back, Jackson?"

Jackson said smoothly, "Just a few moments ago, sir. I'm sorry, if I was needed."

Wentworth shook his head, patted a yawn and ushered Chartres into the living room.

"Kirkpatrick will be here in a few moments," Chartres said quietly. "Meantime, you will not object if I make a nitrogen test of your hands? It might perhaps clear you of suspicion once and for all in the Spider case."

Wentworth looked down at his hands, curiously. "Nitrogen test? Oh, you mean to see if I have been firing a gun? I'd like to take advantage of the alibi, *M'sieur* Chartres, but I'm afraid it won't help." His voice was not louder, but it had a curiously penetrating quality. He hoped that Ram Singh would hear it in the corridor where he had posted him. "The fact is that I indulge in a bit of target practice almost every night before retiring. You

67

will still find the targets I used in place in my soundproofed private pistol range here!"

"Even when you were so tired, *M'sieur* Wentworth?" Chartres' brows were skeptical.

Wentworth smiled and observed, "Oh, I like to keep my hand in, you know. It's one thing I never miss!"

Chartres was already moving toward the doorway, asking, "Could I see these targets, *M'sieur* Wentworth? I am interested to discover the quality of your marksmanship!"

Wentworth nodded with equal casualness. "Why certainly," he said. "You won't mind if Jackson shows you to the range, will you? The truth is, I need something to wake me up."

Chartres, at the doorway, turned sharply. "If it would not be too much imposition, *M'sieur* Wentworth," he said. "I would like the pleasure of your own company!"

Wentworth shrugged and moved slowly toward the doorway. It had been only a trifling delay, but he thought that it would accomplish its purpose. But if Ram Singh had not heard….

At the door of the pistol range, which was set up in the gymnasium, Wentworth did not hesitate at all. He swung the portal wide and gestured to Chartres. He did not even glance inside the range, but turned to press a wall button and throw on the lights.

Chartres sauntered in. *"Ma foi!"* he exclaimed. "You must indeed use your range a great deal. The odor of cordite—it does not dissipate itself! One might almost say a gun had been fired here within the last few minutes!"

Wentworth knew the undertone of suspicion in Chartres'

voice well, by now. "You are entirely right," he acknowledged equably.

Chartres whirled toward him. "I am sorry—you said?"

Wentworth smiled and explained, "That you were right, *M'sieur*. From the odor, one would think a gun had been fired here within the last few minutes. It is a persistent odor, this cordite, eh?"

A SLIGHT flush touched Chartres cheeks, and he eyed the target affixed at the end of the long room. "You group your shots well," he said stiffly.

"I have done better," Wentworth said quietly. "One of these is a little outside the bull's-eye." As he spoke, he stepped to a rack against the wall and lifted down a long-barreled target revolver, snapped open the gate.

Chartres' breath hissed in as Wentworth spun it on a finger, and Wentworth's eyes rested casually on those of the Frenchman.

"But this is murder!" gasped Chartres.

"That's what my friends all say," Wentworth said airily. "They can't stand the competition!" He pivoted toward the target, and the muzzle of the revolver bobbed to the casual contractions of his trigger finger. The racketing shots blended together in a continuous roll of sound. At the end of the shooting, Wentworth turned and replaced the revolver on the rack. Chartres' face had a grayish tinge.

"*Foi de gentilhomme!*" he gasped. "You placed the entire six bullets within the punctures made by your other shots! And such rapidity! Such ease…" He caught himself up, and the slow, hard smile came back into his eyes. *"M'sieur,* I hope we never meet in a duel of guns!"

Wentworth's smile matched his own. It was of the eyes only. "One cannot always choose his enemies," he said smoothly. "The face of fate, of death, is without expression!"

Chartres stiffened, then said, "What do you mean by that, *M'sieur?*" he snapped. "Do you refer to my—"

"Not at all," Wentworth murmured. "You mistake me. I was thinking of a report I heard from an associate tonight. The Underworld is saying that the Brand cannot smile, cannot show any facial expression at all. I think you will agree that his is the face of death itself!... Shall we return to the drawing room, *M'sieur?* I fancy that Kirkpatrick has arrived here at last."

Chartres stood very stiffly through the time that Wentworth took three casual steps toward the door. His voice came out, without strain. "I want to understand you fully," he said slowly. "I think there is an implication there that does not sit well with my honor."

Beside the door, Wentworth faced him steadily. "Why search beneath the words, Chartres?" he asked quietly. "Men of proven courage, like yourself, sir, do not need to challenge the words of... a friend. After you, sir." He gestured toward the door. Then he seemed merely to be making conversation, as Chartres moved toward the doorway slowly. "In America, the duel underwent a curious transformation. During the last fifty years or so of its existence, the pistol entirely replaced the sword...."

Chartres passed Wentworth stiffly, then pivoted to face him. "It would not stop me, you understand, your skill with the pistol!"

Wentworth laughed lightly. "Why, *M'sieur* Chartres!" he exclaimed. "Only enemies fight duels!"

There was no more said before they entered the drawing room, where Kirkpatrick awaited them impatiently. His eyes shuttled keenly between the faces of the two men.

BEFORE HE could speak, Wentworth said offhandedly, "Kirk, I think I can save you a lot of time that's being wasted on this case. Manifestly, when the Spider appears, you have resolved to check on my whereabouts. Hereafter, I will save you the time! I shall remain at your side for the duration of this case!"

Kirkpatrick's frown lightened. "That's splendid, Dick!" he cried. "Quite aside from this checking-up, as you call it, I shall be more than glad of your help. This Brand is a fiend!"

Wentworth caught at one word in Kirkpatrick's speech, and a coldness ran through him. He had thought he would be entirely free to make such a promise, since he believed he had eliminated the Brand. But Kirkpatrick said, "The Brand *is* a fiend!" Was he sure then that the Brand still lived? But that would make Wentworth's own course incredibly difficult. The Spider would not cease his battle against the Brand while he lived—and he could not now withdraw his pledge to Kirkpatrick! But God in heaven, how could he do both those things!

When Chartres spoke, his voice was carefully without offense, despite its overtone of mockery. "An amiable promise, my dear *M'sieur* Wentworth," he said, "but I don't believe that now you will find it difficult to fulfill."

Wentworth turned toward him stiffly, a question in his mind.

His eyes met those of the Frenchman challengingly, and Chartres continued with a challenging glint in his gaze.

"The radio informed me," he said dryly, "that the Brand was dead—under the seal of the Spider!"

Kirkpatrick's tone was grim. "We found a dead man all right, with the Spider's seal on him, and he was dressed in the robes and mask the Brand is reported to wear. Then, within ten minutes, the Brand struck again! No mistaking the powerful weapon he uses! He blew in the walls of a bank, burst open the safe and escaped with almost a half million dollars! A watchman and two of my boys were killed!"

Kirkpatrick's voice was heavy, slow; and the words were like individual blows on Wentworth's heart.

"No," said Kirkpatrick, "the Brand is not dead!"

CHAPTER 5
MURDER MANSION

WENTWORTH SHOOK his head over the news of the Brand's bank robbery, dropped into a chair and signaled Jackson to bring drinks.

"That won't last," he said steadily. "The Brand does not care for open crime, and he must have been desperate indeed after the Spider's expose of him to have committed this robbery. I think the Spider has stopped the present phase of the Brand's activities. I think that there will be a new development very soon that will indicate what his new avenue of murder is."

Kirkpatrick stood peering intently down upon him. "What new development?" he asked softly.

Wentworth shook his head. "We can only wait and see. But after tonight's broadcast, it will have to be something that he can contrive almost single-handed. The Underworld will be too afraid of him, and I hope he will be afraid of the Underworld!"

Chartres said softly, "I take it then that you approve of the Spider's work. You believe he has accomplished a great deal!"

Wentworth's smile was faint. "A man must always approve of his own work," he said.

Chartres stiffened. "Is this a confession?"

Wentworth's smile widened. "The device used by the Spider is one I myself have employed on occasion," he said.

Kirkpatrick broke in impatiently. "Let's have an end of this sparring," he said. "You have no guess, Dick, as to what new course the Brand will follow? You are basing your guess only on the Spider's broadcast?"

"That's right." Wentworth nodded. "I see it something like this: The Brand will find a new way to commit murder for hire, and will probably pick his own customers and give them no chance to refuse. It will be something that he can handle practically alone. I do not think it will be long delayed. He is an impatient man, and his ego is such that he cannot bear to be balked. By morning—"

"By morning!" Kirkpatrick echoed. "I could hope you were wrong, Dick, but you have an uncanny way of being right about the operations of criminals."

Wentworth rose, and his eyes rested sardonically upon those

of Chartres. "Set a thief to catch a thief," he said. "I will be at headquarters first thing in the morning, Kirk."

Wentworth's pose was nonchalant, but there was an inner tension that swelled through his breast. From now on, the Brand would be more cautious—and more terrible! And Wentworth would be terribly hampered in his work by the necessity of working at Kirkpatrick's side as he had promised. Yet in no other way would it be possible to keep Chartres from dogging his footsteps day and night. He would have to find a way... Presently, his callers were gone.

HIS CALL to Nita's home brought her gay voice, and Wentworth felt a part of the weight fall from his heart. "It was a foolish, brave thing you did, my dear," he said. "You might have been hurt in a bad collision, and if those police had been suspicious, they might have opened fire!"

Nita's laughter was a tinkle of silvery bells. "I must find some way to keep you from worrying so much, Dick," she declared. "The only casualty suffered was a summons for reckless driving! I brought my new face home, disguise intact, so that I could duplicate it for the hearing in court. That's the real tragedy. I can't imagine myself going out in daylight with that makeup!"

Wentworth was smiling as he turned toward his bedroom, though well he knew that most of Nita's cheerfulness was assumed to lighten his own burdens. Even that could not lift for long the weight of his apprehensions. Tomorrow, at the latest, the Brand would strike again—and meantime, there was not even a cold trail which gave any hope of leading to the hideout of this harbinger of frightfulness, the Brand!

It was a weary day that followed at police headquarters. There were a half dozen alarms that produced nothing as, following Wentworth's recommendations, the police worked their stool pigeons and tried to squeeze information from other less accessible criminals while the fear of the Brand was still hot in their minds. It was when Kirkpatrick was shuffling through the last sheaf of reports of the day, while winter dusk was gathering, that the break came.

It seemed slight enough at first. Kirkpatrick looked up with a faint smile. "Old Wilson Prender has weakened," he said. "His son won't go to Sing Sing tomorrow."

Wentworth had been staring bleakly out at the drab, windy street. At Kirkpatrick's words, he turned sharply.

"If Wilson Prender has weakened, it won't be the first time," he said. "He's been very patient with that useless young Willie. And there is no question but that the boy was guilty of forging his father's name. What's the story now?"

Kirkpatrick said, "All I have here is a notice from the District Attorney's office that there will be no need to assign a man to take William Prender to Sing Sing tomorrow. It's annotated, 'legal action.' It's evident that old Prender has relented at the last moment and is going to sponsor an appeal."

Wentworth was not looking at Kirkpatrick, but there was a keenness about his face, and his eyes were tightened in speculation. "I'll call the D.A. if you don't mind," he snapped. He caught up the phone, flung a number at the operator. While he waited, he tossed swift words at Kirkpatrick. "This is just a crazy hunch: You recall the rumor that old Prender was planning to change his will? I doubt if he has done so, yet... I'm thinking of the Brand—who performs murders for hire!"

Kirkpatrick shook his head. "Willie Prender has been pretty wild," he said, "but he wouldn't conspire to kill his own father!"

WENTWORTH SHOOK his head impatiently. "Waxy Matthews didn't hire the Brand either, but he paid, and... Hello, Toley? Wentworth... speaking from Kirkpatrick's office. Could you tell me what attorney is acting for young Prender, and who engaged him? No... nothing's wrong, as far as I know...."

Kirkpatrick rose, commenced striding up and down the office. "It would fulfill the conditions you laid down, Dick," he said rapidly. "Murder for hire, and a job that would not require many allies, but—"

"Thomas Burden?" Wentworth was repeating the lawyer's name into the phone. "That's not Wilson Prender's attorney, is it?... I thought not. You say he showed up at the jail and said the boy had sent for him, eh? Now: *Had the prisoner sent for Burden?*"

Kirkpatrick ceased his pacing. When the door of his office opened, he whipped about with the tautness of overstrained nerves. But it was only Raoul Chartres. The Frenchman murmured an apology, his intelligent eyes resting on Wentworth.

"My recommendation is this, Toley," Wentworth was saying. "I think you should compel Thomas Burden to reveal what papers young Prender signed. I think you will find that he signed... an assignment of his share of his father's estate! You will find, further, that Burden either will not know the man for

In that split instant Wentworth saw the doomed group!

whom he is acting, or he will refuse to say! Yes, something pretty big, Toley… You've no doubt heard of the Brand?"

Wentworth snapped the phone back into its cradle, snatched it up again. "Get Wilson Prender on the phone," he ordered. "I want him in person, and you'll probably locate him at his Long Island estate. Speed is essential."

As he finished speaking, Kirkpatrick snapped open the key on his desk annunciator and issued an order: "Send my car to the door at once," he said. "Get Lieutenant Larson of the Nassau police on the wire, and have him stand by."

Chartres sighed audibly. "And I was looking forward to a night of relaxation," he said. "I was prepared to ask you to be my guests at Pierre's. The cuisine there… ah, superb!"

"The Brand is cooking up another dish for us," Wentworth said quietly. "Kirk, you see how the thing points? This lawyer, Thomas Burden, is either in the Brand's employ—or in his power. He obtains from young Prender an assignment of the kid's inheritance—in the future. Actually, Burden may charge any fee for getting Prender out of jail. And apparently, he's claiming a slice of old man Prender's estate, on contingency! The Brand will now kill old Prender—and then bleed Burden. See what I mean?"

"If Thomas Burden really obtained such an assignment, I certainly see it," the commissioner acknowledged. He stood with his hands knotted behind him, waiting tensely.

The phone tingled, and Wentworth snatched up the instrument. "Yes… yes, Mr. Prender. Richard Wentworth, speaking from the commissioner's office. This is a life and death matter, and I do not use the term lightly. Have you authorized your attorneys to make an appeal for your son? Yes, the wire is noisy. I said—" Wentworth broke off, his eyes widening, and his voice took on the crisp, sharp note of command. "Mr. Prender, touch some metal object near you and tell me if you don't feel a definite electric shock. *It may mean your life!*"

Silence hung heavy in the office. Kirkpatrick was suddenly leaning across the desk. Chartres watched with a faint air of amusement. Wentworth's knuckles were white as they gripped the phone.

"I thought so!" he cried. "Mr. Prender, listen carefully. You have read of these murders by the man they call the Brand? That electric shock you received is a proof that he is preparing to kill you! There is just one chance! Turn out every light in your house at once, and get outside in the darkness! Keep out of sight! Believe me, Mr. Prender, your life is at stake. I said…." Wentworth's face was pale beneath the tan, as he turned toward Kirkpatrick. "Get the Nassau police there as fast as you can, Kirk. The static on this wire is growing every moment! I'm afraid I can't make him understand!" He whipped back to the phone, drove heavily stressed words into the transmitter. "Get out of the house! You are going to be murdered! Get out of the house! *You are going to be murdered! Get out of—!*"

Wentworth broke off, dropped the phone into its cradle and heard Kirkpatrick snapping rapid instructions to the Nassau police over another phone. Then Kirkpatrick faced him, his countenance drawn with anxiety. Wentworth shook his head.

"I don't think I got the message over," Wentworth said.

"Prender started shouting, and slammed up the phone. The static was incredibly severe. We've got to get there fast! Kirk, my car is faster than yours, even without the siren we can get there sooner."

THEY WERE striding from the office, with Chartres trotting along in their wake. There was a secret amusement in his eyes as he sprang into Wentworth's car and Kirkpatrick's orders sent motorcycle police ahead of the limousine, their sirens screaming. Jackson, behind the wheel, wore dark civilian clothing and a pull-down felt very much like Wentworth's. His big hands rode the wheel of the Daimler lightly as it roared from the curb.

"I'm not acquainted with all the details of the matter," Chartres said gently, "but it seems to me that *M'sieur* Wentworth possesses more information concerning the way this death brand works than is contained in the reports of police. Would it be impertinent to inquire how he knows that a preponderance of static electricity indicates that the Brand is about to strike?" He waved a hand deprecatingly at Kirkpatrick's glare. "Do not forget, *M'sieur le Commissionaire,* that it is my duty exclusively to track down this Spider! *M'sieur* Wentworth, would you so much mind replying to my inquiry?"

Wentworth was impatient at the question; felt a tingle of alarm that was not unmixed with admiration. Chartres' mind was keen, and he was clinging unswervingly to his task. His point was well made.

"One might almost say," Wentworth replied easily, "that the thing suddenly hit me. In fact, it fairly leaps to the eye, as you would say. As I pointed out, we are dealing with an implosion.

This means an instantaneous exhaustion of the air in any given area… and I have heard descriptions of the sound made by these implosions. 'Like little thunder' was one simile. Now, only one thing could make a sound like little thunder, and that would be a small bolt of lightning… hence, static electricity!"

"May I compliment you, *m'sieur?* A truly remarkable deduction… based on so little evidence!"

Kirkpatrick shifted impatiently. "You two postpone this quibbling," he said curtly. "More important matters are at hand. Dick, I confess this implosion explanation does not quite satisfy me. The mere exhaustion of air, the creation of a vacuum. At sea level, the pressure is only fifteen pounds to the square inch."

Wentworth smile faintly. "Have you ever experienced a hurricane? They tear up powerful trees by the roots, overturn cars, smack houses from their foundations, scoop up great waves from the surface of the ocean."

Kirkpatrick was still frowning. "They don't make a man explode!"

Wentworth shook his head. He was not looking any longer at his two confreres, but peering ahead, where the headlights of his car slashed the blackness of the night. Jackson was driving well, and the two policemen on motorcycles were slicing the traffic wide open… but how much time did they have? Of one thing Wentworth was sure: The Brand would have to strike in person. He would not trust his equipment to other hands than his own. And the Spider would be there, too!

"In a hurricane," Wentworth said quietly, "there is a decline in pressure of about three pounds. Rarely more than that. In other words, a difference in atmospheric pressure of three pounds can cause such damage as I indicated, by bringing the winds rushing in at terrific force. A hundred and fifty miles an hour and more. The Brand's instrument *exhausts* the air in any given area; in other words, a drop from fifteen pounds—to zero!" The smile on his lips was pallid, bitter. "If you can imagine the force of ten hurricanes, a wind of ten times the force of a hurricane, concentrated in an area the size of a room, you will understand something of the power of the implosion!"

Kirkpatrick uttered a strangled oath. "I hadn't pictured it that way," he said thickly. "Nothing on earth could stand against it!"

Wentworth said slowly, "So far, *nothing has!*"

Even Chartres was silent, and the rush of the wind, the shriek of the sirens, beat on the ears of the three men, as the car sliced through the darkness. "Faster, Jackson!" Wentworth snapped. "Give those motorcycle men the horn!"

THE DAIMLER'S horn blasted twice, and the taillights of the motorcycles pulled ahead. The whine of the wind increased. Trees beside the car twisted like the figures of a tortured dream.

Wentworth turned his thin smile toward Kirkpatrick. "We are doing a little over ninety," he called above the wind. "Much less than the speed of a hurricane!"

But Wentworth's mind was intent on the battle ahead. Chartres had given ample evidence that he intended to concentrate on the Spider to the exclusion of any other work, no matter what the circumstances. He could count on the man keeping keen watch over him, and Wentworth did not intend to be hampered! At whatever cost, he must seize this opportunity to be rid of the Brand once and for all! Each time the Brand made his appearance, men died—and so far it was only in his attacks upon humanity that Wentworth had been able to make contact. This time he must make sure, at whatever cost to himself.

Wentworth's gaze centered on Jackson. Deliberately, he had dressed Jackson in clothing similar to his own. The suits and hats were not quite the same color, but with Jackson's able imitation of his employer's movements, he would pass as Wentworth. That was the only protection on which he could rely. If it failed… Wentworth shook his head grimly. Regardless of that danger, he must finish the Brand this night!

"The Nassau police should be there ahead of us," Kirkpatrick muttered. "It is a question of whether they will be able to persuade Prender to do as Wentworth directed. He is a stubborn man."

Wentworth made no answer, and the car heeled over in a sharp swing to the right. Jackson's shoulder muscles bunched with the effort to straighten out again and, almost immediately, he was braking to cut between high white stone columns. The motorcycles of the two police couriers swerved aside, and the heavy Daimler raced on, accelerating up a long curving grade that climbed a sloping lawn.

"The house is beyond the crest of the hill," Kirkpatrick said stiffly. "We should see the lights in a moment!"

"In a moment…" Wentworth repeated. "But we should be seeing the roof already. *God, what is that sound!*"

It pierced even through the moan of the engine, through the whimper of the wind, and it was shrill and wailing and terri-

83

ble—a woman's cry of utter grief and desolation! The car swept over the rise, and Jackson brought the heavy limousine to a sudden halt. The headlights stabbed through the aisles of the trees, and their merciless glare picked out a scene of complete ruin. Where the enormous stone mansion of Wilson Prender had stood, there was a gaping crater in the raw earth; strewn across it was a jumble of masonry and tortured beams. A dozen huge trees that had towered graciously above the mansion had been yanked from their roots and tossed like jackstraws across the debris!

"Ten hurricanes," Wentworth said slowly. "But I heard a cry...."

As he spoke, a man in the blue uniform of the Nassau County Police stepped into the headlights and waved an arm in a slow, heavy movement as if incredible weights were attached to his limbs. Two other men followed him, and one of those wore police blue, while the other was the short, dynamic figure of Wilson Prender. He walked like a man who has taken a heavy blow, yet still has the courage to stand. His head was up, and his hands, swinging at his sides, were knotted into fists. Behind them, a man, coatless in the cold, helped a weeping woman....

Wentworth snapped forward. "Lights off, Jackson!" he called. He slammed open the door. "Run!" he shouted. "Run for your lives!"

BEHIND HIM, he heard Kirkpatrick's startled oath, but Wentworth already was on the earth, sprinting forward. "Run!" he shouted again. "Run! There may be another blast!"

He heard men swear in dazed uncertainty and, even while

Wentworth hurled himself forward, there was a crackling among the trees as if a strong wind stirred there, and across the path of the car there flickered a thin blue-white flame! It streaked a lance-line of brilliance through the darkness and, in that weird illumination, the startled group of refugees from ruin stood out in awful clarity. Only one of them had started to run, and he had barely taken the first stride. Wilson Prender stood rock-still, head up, fists clenched in defiance!

For that split-instant, Wentworth saw the group and then the light had gone out, swallowed in the tearing crash of thunder. Wentworth felt the concussion strike him in a wave of air that swayed him. He staggered, caught his balance against a tree trunk.

"Out of the car!" he called hoarsely. "Out of it and scatter before there is another implosion!"

He heard the hard beat of feet striking the frozen ground, a smothered curse in French. Kirkpatrick's voice called a hoarse query.

"What happened to them?" he cried. "There hasn't been a sound out of them, and—"

There was another of those whispering blue-white streaks through the midnight blackness of the woods. Mingled with the crash of the implosion, there was the wrenching groan of twisted metal, the hissing blast of exploding tires. Kirkpatrick's voice pinched off, but presently Wentworth's straining ears heard it again, heard his whispered curses. Wentworth pushed away from the tree.

"No lights, if you love life!" he whispered, and his voice carried piercingly through the dead quiet of those winter woods. Somewhere a tree creaked dryly, released from the implosion's tug. "No light, but follow me! There's only one place those bolts could have come from! Only one place that commands this entire scene. See, against the sky... that old farm house on the knoll!"

Jackson's voice was suddenly quiet beside him, a whisper that barely reached his ears. "Orders, Major?" he asked.

Wentworth's hand clamped on his in the darkness, and the swift pressure of his fingers, using international code, dribbled out his message. "Stay close... out of sight. I'll want you to lead Chartres astray. Later, say you went to the road to watch for escaping cars."

Jackson's hand dropped from his, and Wentworth was bounding forward. Once more he whispered, "This way! Kirk, you all right? Chartres? Jackson?" Their murmured assents reached him, but he was already sprinting toward the farmhouse a full five hundred yards away through the dark woods. Now that the glare of headlights, the blinding brilliance of the Brand, was gone, the crisp clear frostiness of the stars spangled out against the sky. The gaunt silhouettes of the winter-stripped trees were like the bars of a giant prison window. Through them, Wentworth wove a swift way. He heard the beat of running feet beside and behind him.

"No hope for those poor devils," Kirkpatrick panted.

Wentworth said, "None at all. The bolt went straight into their midst." His voice sounded dry, rasping. "The car was folded up like a cardboard box under the tire of a twenty-ton truck."

A RAVINE threw its chasm across their path, and progress

was difficult in the dark. Thorns stabbed Wentworth's flesh, and the brook at the bottom made a cold tinkling like ice in a broken glass. Chartres continued to swear in a mild, exasperated voice. They were across, and surging over the brink nearest the farmhouse. It was very close, less than a hundred yards, and Wentworth led to the cover of a small grove of trees.

"I'll take the back," Wentworth whispered. "Kirk—"

"Yes," Kirkpatrick whispered. "I'm armed. They're bound to leave soon, if they haven't already."

Chartres said, irritably, "They would not be such fools as to wait!"

Wentworth turned on his heel without further words and plunged into a thicket from which he had caught a whisper of sound. Jackson had tapped two small rocks together. Leaping into the thicket, Wentworth stumbled forward.

"Go ahead, Jackson!" he whispered. "Run for the road over the hill. Watch yourself!"

Jackson was already up and running and, against the pale sky, his posture was exactly that of Richard Wentworth. Chartres swore in his wake, and Kirkpatrick was circling toward the front of the house. Through a long moment, Wentworth lay silent in the brush, and then he was gliding silently across the stretch of hummocked grass that separated him from the farm building. His eyes already had spotted his goal. Each of the blank windows of the house gave back the cold glitter of the stars, all except one! Wentworth nodded to himself as he stole forward. He thought he would find the Brand there! The crime king would not have fled without making sure of his kills, and certainly he had not advanced toward the ruins of the Prender mansion!

Wentworth was a shadow among other shadows, silent and invisible. In his fist he carried the coiled length of the silken Web, and he half rose presently against the building's side. His arm whipped upward. There was a tap as the line settled about the chimney, no more. Then Wentworth was climbing!

The creak of cautious feet upon the rotted boards of the porch told him that Kirkpatrick was already on his way into the building! He longed to shout a warning, but smothered the cry. It was not of his own peril he thought; of facing the Brand's murder weapon; of being caught in the role of the Spider! But Kirkpatrick was terribly vulnerable… The front door creaked open!

Wentworth took a final handhold on the silken line, seized his automatic in his other fist and—swung wide out from the side of the house! For an instant, his swinging body was silhouetted against the sky, and then he swung back toward the building again and flung himself bodily through the window!

From the black cavern of the room, flame stabbed toward him, but it was the orange-red thrust of a gunshot! Wentworth felt the hot breath of lead whip past his ear, then he pitched to the floor. He hit the floor on his knees and a cautious hand; then he was instantly erect and against the wall. Once more, gun flame cut the thick darkness of the room, probing toward the spot where he had fallen. Wentworth's gun was lifted and ready. His lips parted, and laughter gusted from his lips, laughter flat and mocking and terrible… the laughter of the Spider! The crash of his gunshot seemed to punch the walls outward, let them slam back inward. The whole house seemed to rock with the concussion. A body slammed against the wall, then to the floor with a dull thud.

FROM BELOW, on the stairs, came Kirkpatrick's wild shout, the sound of his feet on the steps. Guns were crashing in the distance, too, hammering in the woods to which he had dispatched Jackson. The devil! Were he and Chartres dueling, or… or had the Brand already sped that way before they arrived!

Wentworth swore and switched on the cold beam of a pocket flashlight. It glanced across the huddle of a man's body on the floor, the scalp gleaming with wiry red hair, and with something else red that flowed from the hole Wentworth's lead had bored. Wentworth rolled him over on his back. For the moment, the rapid rush of Kirkpatrick's charge, the hammer of those shots in the woods, faded from his consciousness. He was bitterly disappointed. Once more he had killed and had bagged only one of the Brand's gunmen. This man's heavy face was a rougher duplicate of that other gunman he had slain in the robes of the Brand. Apparently, the Brand was served by brothers.

Fiercely, Wentworth stooped over the body, and his hand flicked to his vest pocket and ground the base of his cigarette lighter against the forehead of that shattered skull. A long leap, then, and he had reached the window! He had intended to kill quietly here and then take up his stand again behind the building. All hope of that was gone now, for Kirkpatrick had reached the door. He peered toward the woods, where the guns had ceased to crash. The hum of a speeding auto came to his ears… but it was not that he sought.

A small, racing figure that could only be Chartres, was sprinting back toward the building. The Frenchman had discovered the trick with Jackson and, with the tenacity of his breed, was returning in the hope of trapping Wentworth in the Spider's role!

In a single bound, Wentworth sprang from the window sill and slid down the silken rope. At the same instant, he blasted lead and flame from his automatic toward a clump of bushes near the woods! He compressed the safety grip. Then, locking it in place with a special catch, he tossed the automatic far from him toward that same clump of bushes. The gun slammed to earth, and flame leaped from its muzzle, exactly if some man hidden there had returned his fire!

The next instant Wentworth had reached the ground and was racing toward that clump of bushes. He fired twice more with his second automatic. From the window behind him, flame reached out into the darkness, and he heard Kirkpatrick's voice shout clearly.

"Stop him! Stop him, Dick!" he cried. "It's the Spider!"

In the next instant, Wentworth plunged into the clump of shrubbery. He fired two more shots, threshed around in the bushes as if two men battled there.

"I've got him, Kirk!" he shouted. "I've got him. The Spider is—"

He cut that cry off in its midst, as if a blow had stopped the words in his throat, and afterward there floated across the darkness the mocking laughter of the Spider! Crouched low in the shrubbery, Wentworth grimly took the one chance that was left to him. He stiffened the fingers of his right hand and deliberately jabbed them into the nerve centers of his throat. There was a flash of excruciating pain just before he plunged into darkness....

CHAPTER 6
VOICE OF DOOM

DRIFTING BACK from the unconsciousness into which he had deliberately plunged himself, Wentworth heard the voices of Kirkpatrick and Chartres in sharp argument.

"I tell you," Kirkpatrick said angrily, "that I am willing to swear there were two men fighting here in the bushes. Wentworth apparently had hold of the Spider. I heard him cry out to that effect, and then his voice broke off. The Spider laughed—and we find Wentworth unconscious. You cannot dispute that he is unconscious!"

Chartres' tones were cold. "I cannot, *M'sieur le Commissionaire*," he said. "Nor can I dispute your evidence, if you are convinced this is what you saw. Yet Wentworth deliberately misled me, sent me off after this man of his, this Jackson, while he stayed behind!"

Kirkpatrick's voice changed to impatience. "Wentworth is precisely where he said he would be, watching the back of the house. As for Jackson, Wentworth placed him wisely, since the two of you almost caught the Brand before he reached his auto." Wentworth heard Kirkpatrick step close to him, felt the solicitude in his friend's manner as he bent toward him.

91

Wentworth stirred heavily. "Hurry," he whispered. "Have to hurry!"

Kirkpatrick's voice was gentle. "It's all right, old man. Just take it easy. You were knocked out!"

Wentworth's urge for action was genuine. His mind already grasped the next step that the Brand would take, and it filled him with apprehension. Damn it, he should have taken care of this before he left the city—and yet he had not been sure then that the Brand actually would strike. It had been pure deduction. He tossed, tried desperately to thrust himself upward.

"Hurry, Kirk," he muttered. "Must get to phone, then back to New York!"

Kirkpatrick's arm was strong beneath his shoulders. "What's the matter?" he asked quietly.

Wentworth had his eyes open now, though the agony of his shocked nerve centers sent pulsing waves of pain through his skull. Chartres was watching him narrowly, though his eyes were shadowed in the darkness where they stood.

"That lawyer, and young Prender," Wentworth said.

"I'll take care of the lawyer," Kirkpatrick said grimly.

Wentworth shook his head, took a single stride and stood swaying while he fought for full control of his senses. "You don't understand," he said. "It isn't enough to arrest the lawyer, or to keep Prender in jail. Since we anticipated this attack, the Brand must realize we saw through his operations in New York. No jail will protect Prender or the lawyer from him, for he must shut their mouths at once! That bolt of his… The only possible protection will be to hide them where they can't be found!"

"You're right," Kirkpatrick agreed harshly. "Jackson, I don't think Mr. Wentworth can walk very well yet. There should be a police car somewhere near the house that hasn't been destroyed. Could you get it, drive around by the road? It's only a hundred yards from here!"

Jackson's hand flew up in salute. "Right away, sir!" He ran off into the darkness, and Kirkpatrick, watching him go, turned to Chartres. "I don't see how you could have mistaken his stride for that of Wentworth," he said gruffly.

Chartres' voice was mild as he turned toward the road. "It is just possible," he said, "that Jackson does not always carry himself the same way."

A FEW moments after they reached the road, Jackson brought a police car to a halt beside them and flung wide the door. His jaw was set, and there was pallor about his wide eyes. "God, sir, you wouldn't believe what that flash of light did to the Daimler. It's folded up like a collapsible box. And those poor people...."

Kirkpatrick nodded stiffly. "I've seen the work of those bolts before. No one survived?"

Jackson said thickly, "Not one!"

The four men were crowded in the narrow coupé, but Jackson did not check his swift pace on that account. The coupé howled down the grades, and the roar of its engine split the night. Wentworth leaned forward stiffly to switch on the radio. It came alive in the middle of what was plainly a long repeated broadcast.

"... Reams, call headquarters. Sergeant Reams, call headquarters. All cars are ordered to relay this call. Sergeant Reams, call headquarters..." It was the code call for Kirkpatrick himself!

93

Kirkpatrick smothered an exclamation. "It must be important, damn it. I would have to be isolated at a time like this."

"There's a police booth near," Wentworth said quietly. His eyes strained ahead through the night. It was apparent that his ruse had succeeded in concealing the fact that he was the Spider, though it had far from allayed the suspicions of Chartres. That became unimportant beside the necessity of finding and hiding the lawyer and young Prender. They might possess a clue to the Brand!

The green lights that marked the roadside police booth sprang into sight, and presently Jackson pulled up beside it. Kirkpatrick was out instantly, striding toward the booth. The booth was locked… but Kirkpatrick did not even hesitate. His long-barreled revolver leaped to his hand, and the lock was shattered by a single shot.

Wentworth leaned stiffly against the side of the car, waiting. Chartres faced him. "You wouldn't mind surrendering your guns for a ballistics test, would you, *M'sieur* Wentworth? You see, I consider *M'sieur* Kirkpatrick a little… prejudiced!"

Wentworth turned, and found himself peering into a small, deadly automatic that jutted toward his heart.

"There are no objections," he said coldly. "But there was a remark made which I did not care for, *M'sieur* Chartres. I request that you retract it at once! Kirkpatrick would not swerve from his duty to save his own life, much less a guilty friend's."

"And yet it seems to me," Chartres began, "that the eyesight of *M'sieur* Kirkpatrick—"

Wentworth said softly, "I have warned you!"

Chartres shrugged slightly, "As you will, but I should like to have those guns at once!"

Wentworth was aware that Jackson was ready to strike down the Frenchman if he were given even a hint of a signal, and there was no question but that Wentworth was in a bad spot. One gun would match certainly with the bullet in the body of the dead gunman upon whose forehead was printed the seal of the Spider! Yet he could not refuse to surrender it. Wentworth bowed slightly, and crossed his hands to his guns. He withdrew them slowly. Under the circumstances, his eyes staring directly into the gaze of Chartres, it was not strange that one of the guns fell from his hands and struck, muzzle first upon the concrete pavement. He knew he had dropped the gun which had most recently wrought death.

Wentworth uttered a sharp oath, and stooped swiftly. He picked up the gun and once more, beneath the running board of the car, banged the muzzle down heavily upon the concrete. When he straightened, his face was grave, but there was laughter behind his eyes.

"I'm afraid I've spoiled your evidence for you, *M'sieur* Chartres," he said regretfully. "You are no doubt aware that a defect at the muzzle, such as might be caused by a fall, would make it impossible to match bullets from this weapon. It would give quite another series of markings!"

FOR ONCE, Chartres' self-control snapped. His lips shrank back from his teeth in a hissing oath, but before he could speak, or reach out for the guns, Kirkpatrick bounded from the booth.

"Too late, Dick!" he snapped angrily. "They've already got

both young Prender and that lawyer! And the warden was killed with them! Damn it, this man must be stopped. He *must!* He is—" He stopped, staring at the guns in Wentworth's hand; at the small, efficient weapon held by Chartres. "What is this?" he demanded.

Chartres forced himself to be calm, holstered his automatic. "Further trickery," he sputtered. "I demand his guns to check with the bullet in the body of the slain man, and he deliberately drops one so that it strikes on the muzzle; so that ballistics tests will show nothing!"

Wentworth shrugged. "I regret dropping the gun. It could not be helped, as *M'sieur* Chartres should be the first to agree. I am more than willing to surrender the guns!"

Kirkpatrick's jaw was grim. "I will make no comment on your demand, Chartres," he said curtly, "but it is scarcely good judgment to allow a test gun to be so damaged. In this country, we train our officers in those little niceties."

Chartres drew himself up, and there was anger burning in his eyes. But before he could speak, Kirkpatrick pounded on, and there was a dark flush on his cheekbones. "There will be no more of this for tonight," he said flatly. "I have other matters, and more important ones to attend to, than this ceaseless attempt to humiliate Wentworth! Did you understand me? Three men have been murdered inside the jail, and by the Brand—"

"In my country," Chartres interrupted, "such things do not occur. We train our officers in those little niceties!"

For an instant, anger scored Kirkpatrick's face, then he laughed ruefully. "I deserved that. My apologies, Chartres. Now let's have done with this bickering and get to work! How in the name of heaven the Brand got back to the city so quickly...."

"We are near the water," Wentworth said quietly. "A seaplane, perhaps. Shall we get under way?"

They climbed into the narrow confines of the coupé again, and Jackson wheeled it toward the city. Chartres sat completely silent, but Wentworth began to talk above the rush of the wind and the roar of the motor.

"The Brand has once more stopped our inquiries," he said, "unless we can trace him through that dead man."

Kirkpatrick shook his head. "It was one of the three brothers, and the other two already have been killed by the Spider. They were merely crooks for hire. We can assume that the Brand hired them to fight his losing battles while he escaped!"

Wentworth nodded gravely. "The Brand has escaped us, but the field is narrowing. His criminal allies have been destroyed, and he himself has been forced out of the alliance he sought with the Underworld. I think we can easily put a stop to this latest campaign of his, which plainly was undertaken without adequate preparation. To collect through young Prender's inheritance would be a slow job. It takes a year to probate a will in this state. If you can persuade District Attorney Toley to publicize the fact that he will fight probate of any will in which the death has occurred by means of the Brand's bolt, I think we will stop the Brand there also!"

Kirkpatrick said slowly, "We only force him to find some new field of operations. Perhaps it would be better to allow him to work where we can find him!"

"You'll find him only after he has killed his victims," Wentworth said emphatically. "It was only good luck that we were in this case as early as we were—and our sole accomplishment was to add a number of policemen to the victims! No, Kirk, we must continue to drive the Brand from every barricade until he is finally pushed to the wall and captured… or killed!"

Wentworth's voice rang with challenge, and when he fell silent no man spoke. The loudness of the gusty wind and the laboring engine crept into the closeness of the coupé. The headlights rolled back the darkness, but it swept in behind them again, ran beside them in dark secret menace. Ahead, somewhere, the Brand already had struck, might strike again and again without hindrance as long as the fiercely murderous bolt remained his exclusive possession. There was no defense!

WENTWORTH FOUGHT to wring from his keen brain some clue to the next attack. The Brand would get no profit from the Prender fiasco, and he must realize that all such future attempts would be abortive, so far as collecting on them was concerned. Wentworth tried to tell himself that he had been successful against the Brand. Twice his swift strokes had driven the Brand from profitable fields, forced him to seek other methods of collecting on his murder weapon. Three of his allies had been killed, and there had been only three men opposed to him on that first night, when he had so narrowly escaped being trapped in the dark alley. Yes, some things he had accomplished… but the Brand remained at large! And, of the future, the Spider could be sure of only one thing:

The Brand would strike again!

The radio beneath the coupé's cowling whined thinly, and Wentworth leaned forward to turn up the amplifier. He stayed that way, frozen by the voice that rasped from the loudspeaker. The Brand was speaking!

"My friends," said the Brand slowly. "Friends of the Brand, you who this night received... *gifts*... from me!"

Kirkpatrick's oath rang out harshly, but Wentworth's hand, resting on his arm, stilled his outbreak. They listened in an aching silence.

"There will be further gifts," the Brand went on softly. "Of course I will require some slight service from you in the future. I know you fear me, thanks to the efforts of my dear, dear friend, the Spider—and you do well to fear me! But profits will flow from my hands, and those who are faithful need not fear the Brand! See that you heed the summons when it comes... tomorrow night! Obey—*or fear the Brand!*"

THE NEXT day, the newspapers shrieked demands that the Brand be captured, be destroyed. Even the headlines of Europe's travails were crowded to a minor display by the horrors of the carnage on the Prender estate and within the city jail.

"None of us is safe from this terror!" enunciated Julius Iron-wanger, the famous radio commentator, the next night. "The very walls which would protect us, even from enemy bombs, become our enemies under this new menace. The creature, who calls himself the Brand, can collapse them about us! He can crush us, even though we sought protection in the prisons of the city!

"The police seem helpless... and they are not to blame. This is beyond their experience, beyond their capacity. And so, I make

99

an appeal! I cry from the depths of the hell into which this terror has plunged us. I appeal to the Spider!… If you are within the sound of my voice, Spider, heed this cry, and you will earn the undying gratefulness of the humanity which you, in your own way, always serve. His voice rose:

"Save us, Spider! Save us from the Brand!"

The voice of the radio commentator echoed through thousands and thousands of homes. The Brand heard it where he sat at ease in his home, and he giggled thinly behind the steel mask he wore even here. In the Underworld, men heard and cursed murderously. And the people hopelessly hoped….

That voice sounded, too, in Kirkpatrick's office, and the commissioner lifted his head from the weary and profitless reports stacked upon his desk. Raoul Chartres' eyes gleamed mockingly—and Wentworth smothered a yawn.

"The capture of the Spider apparently would not be popular now," Wentworth murmured. "I think I shall have a bath and a bit of dinner. *M'sieur* Chartres, will you accompany me—or follow me?"

Chartres lifted a shoulder in a slight shrug, and Kirkpatrick thrust sharply from his chair. He crossed to stare bleakly out the broad window and toward the windy street, where night laid its thick black mantle.

"Eighteen thousand men at work all day," he said harshly, "the entire force of police. And not one of them has turned up a clue even to the receivers of the Brand's gifts, much less to where they will meet with the Brand tonight! It's maddening!"

"Fear makes the best gag," Wentworth said amiably. "You don't need me for an hour or so, eh, Kirk?"

Kirkpatrick swung away from the window, his gaunt figure a rigidly braced silhouette against the blueness of the outside dark. "No suggestions, Dick?"

There was compassion in Wentworth's eyes as he gazed on his friend. The city's travail was passionately his concern. Not even the Spider took such matters more to heart. He was doing all now that the law could accomplish. Only… the Spider could do more….

"Nothing strictly legal, Kirk, "Wentworth said quietly. "A dragnet to bring in all the leading crooks of the city might help, especially those addicted to violence."

Kirkpatrick's eyes were gloomy. "The men we want will be expecting something like that, and they'll keep out of the way. Yet it might be worth a try."

Wentworth turned toward the door. "I'll be at home, if you want me. Coming, Chartres?"

Chartres said smoothly, "I shall leave you to guess about that, *M'sieur* Wentworth. *Au 'voir!*"

BUT WENTWORTH, speeding home behind Jackson, wasted no thoughts on Chartres. During the day, he had made his plans in detail, and they included no return to Kirkpatrick's office in the immediate future. The police had done their best, and failed… It was time for the Master of Men to act!

Wentworth stopped once on the way home, and the limousine waited with lights out on a dark side street. He made a phone call from a booth that stood in a row of fifteen others in constant use. But it was not Wentworth's voice that spoke over the instrument when the call had gone through to an estate far out on Long Island. It was the harsh, fierce whisper of the Brand!

"Sanders," he said, "this is the Brand calling, the Brand, whom all men fear—and obey! You will have a hundred thousand dollars ready for me at ten o'clock tonight, at your home, or you and all with you shall die! Remember what happened to Prender!

"A hundred thousand at ten o'clock... *or fear the Brand!*"

Wentworth clicked the receiver into place over the sputterings of Roscoe Sanders, then he went rapidly to his car. His eyes stabbed along the dark street and failed to spot Chartres in pursuit. But the man was somewhere near, no doubt of that! A thin smile stirred Wentworth's lips in memory of the fright in Sanders' voice, but the man needed such cavalier treatment. A crooked politician, a corrupter of judges, Sanders had for a long time merited the Spider's attention!

Five minutes later, Wentworth was entering his home when he heard Ram Singh's grave voice. "The *sahib* comes now—Kirkpatrick, *sahib!*"

Wentworth took the phone from Ram Singh's hand, and there was a secret smile in his eyes as he listened to Kirkpatrick's exasperation. "I have no choice," the commissioner was saying, "except to go to Sanders' home in person with a strong guard. If I refuse, the mayor will issue orders... and there is a chance that we will catch the Brand there! After all, we have no clue at all to his whereabouts in the city. We are not even sure that he is here!"

Wentworth agreed sombrely. "You're leaving at once? If you don't mind, Kirk, I'll catch a shower and eat first, and then I'll have Ram Singh drive me out and join you there. Right… and good luck, Kirk!"

Wentworth clicked the phone up, and when he turned from it, there was no more of the sombreness in his tones. He snapped orders. "An hour from now, the seaplane is to be warmed up. Jackson, you will ride out to Peconic Bay with Ram Singh—but you will ride in the rear of the limousine in my clothing. You will be followed by Chartres. Peconic is on the road to the Sanders estate!"

Jackson's broad-jawed face parted in a wide grin. "You're going to fly out and meet us there. We'll switch… and Chartres will give you an alibi."

Wentworth nodded crisply. "I'm leaving now, Jackson. Carry on! Ram Singh…."

"Han, sahib!" The powerfully built Sikh bowed his turbaned head.

"Ram Singh, you will be followed. Do not attempt to elude your pursuer… but do not allow him to overtake you!"

"Wah, sahib!" Ram Singh said contemptuously. "If this rabbit of a man overtakes us, I will snap his neck, so!"

Wentworth laughed. "Not that, Ram Singh," he said. "Chartres is a *pukka sahib*. He happens merely to be on the other side of the fence!"

Wentworth whirled away from the two men then, strode rapidly to his dressing room. In the bathroom, he switched on the light over the mirrored medicine cabinet and then picked up a towel. He muffled the light three times in regular sequence, turning it off and on again, extinguishing it finally. The lavatory receded into the wall and Wentworth crouched, then sprang through the opening and allowed the fixture to slide into place again. He was in a compactly arranged dressing room. Clothes swung from racks on the wall, and there was a dressing table with all the articles of disguise which the Spider had devised.

Wentworth set swiftly to work.

Five minutes later, a curious figure limped across the narrow room toward the outer wall. The man was shabbily dressed, and one knee was stiff. Grizzled hair thrust out from beneath a battered hat, and there were hooded spectacles over the eyes. Wentworth had become a man whom all in the Underworld knew: crotchety Blinky McQuade, half-blind ex-safe-blower. Some had laughed at him; and some had feared him, briefly, before they died under the Spider's seal! But his prowess as a safecracker was well known, and he was admitted wherever criminals gathered.

Another secret door let him out on the service stairway of the apartment house. There was a bundle under his arm, and he moved swiftly for all his apparent slowness. His alibi was arranged—for one hour! In that time, the Spider hoped to solve the problem that had baffled eighteen thousand police! In that one hour, the Spider expected to save the city from the Brand! A narrow margin, even for the Master of Men!

THERE WERE two spots called Kelly's. One, with blaring orchestra and colored lights, which the suckers paid to visit; and another, in a basement room where the big men of the underworld came to gamble away a few grand, or to pick up news of an expert they temporarily needed. Blinky McQuade ordinarily lacked the funds for the poker and dice tables, but his standing as an expert on strongboxes was his passport even here.

Tonight, the doorman stared incredulously at Blinky McQuade, whose usual greeting was a curse. Tonight, Blinky actually cracked a sour smile and growled, "Hello, Spike!"

"Jeez, Blinky!" gasped Spike. "Youse must feel swell!"

A few men spoke to Wentworth as he shuffled with McQuade's awkward, stiff-kneed gait across the room. Behind the hooded glasses, his gray-blue eyes were keen. There was a bigger crowd than usual in Kelly's, and there was a certain low tone to the voices; a veiled sideways scrutiny of newcomers that told of the tension that gripped these men—and Wentworth knew he had come to the right place!

There was no doubt in Wentworth's mind that some of the men here had received the summons of the Brand. Hence, the grim tension. Like all other men in peril, they sought the company of their fellows.

It was Wentworth's job now to pick out the men who would tonight meet the Brand face to face! If he could do that— quickly—the Spider would win his battle tonight!

Wentworth sidled up to the dice game and watched the roll of the transparent cubes with his grizzled head bowed. A radio emitted soft music, but when the announcer's voice broke in, everything in that room stopped. The men seemed unconscious of the action, but it told much to Wentworth. The summons, then, would come by radio! But it could not tell the place, of course; only the time. The men must already know the place.

Wentworth made a furtive business of dragging out his wallet, of fingering out a bill into his fist. It was a crisp new one thousand dollar bill that he threw onto the dice table.

"A thousand says he's wrong!" Wentworth said harshly.

Every eye turned speculatively toward Wentworth, but he was not looking at any of them. His eyes quested for the effect among other men of his mention of big money—big money for Blinky McQuade! At a side table, drinking, sat three men who looked at Blinky, and then toward each other.

The dice skipped and bounded across the table top, and the man who had thrown them swore raggedly. "Four straight passes, damn you, Blinky, and then you had to jinx me with that wrong bet!"

Blinky's smile was sour as he scooped up the packet of bills he had won. "You don't look like a winner to me," he said. "Me, this is my lucky night!"

He made three more bets and won them all before the dice were handed to him. He allowed Blinky McQuade one sharp, scornful laugh as he spun the green cubes between his greedy palms. "My lucky night," he rasped. "All right, boys, there's five thousand to fade!"

He was only half intent on the dicing, for his eyes went again to the three men drinking at a corner table. The radio music broke, and the three men's heads swung as one toward the instrument. Afterward, they relaxed... and their glances stole toward Blinky as he warmed the dice. They whispered together. And Wentworth knew. These three, at least, had been summoned by the Brand!

WENTWORTH TURNED his eyes to the table, and rolled the dice. Seven. He laughed sharply, scooped up the cubes as the croupier's rake thrust them toward him.

"Let it ride," he said. "This is Blinky McQuade's lucky night!"

It seemed to be. Four times he let his money ride, and each time rolled a natural or made his point. The fifth time he hesitated, then deliberately drew all his money toward him, save a thousand-dollar bill. And once more, his judgment was justified. He lost the dice.

He turned away from the table, stuffing the great wad of bills into his pockets, and for once the grin on Blinky McQuade's face was not sour.

"Set 'em up!" he rasped at the barkeep. "Set 'em up for the house!"

Wentworth calculated that twenty minutes of his hour was gone, but in that twenty minutes he had achieved more than the entire police force! For he had convinced the three men in the corner that he, too, had received a gift and a summons from the Brand. Where else would Blinky McQuade get money to throw away? Now, his purchase of drinks would give them the opportunity to approach him. That way, they would be unsuspicious, whereas if he went to them, they would be on their guard!

He was aware of the three men closing in behind him, turned suddenly with a snarl. "Keep your hands away from my pockets!" he snapped in Blinky McQuade's harsh voice.

107

"Sure," the leading man smiled. "Sure, Blinky, I'd just like to talk to you a minute! I'm Jack Bosher."

Blinky McQuade's belligerence did not change, but his voice was quieter when he spoke. Bosher was a man to conjure with in the Underworld. Beginning as a fire-eater in a carnival sideshow, Bosher was a Chicago crook with a reputation of having cleaned up millions in a strikebreaking racket—after having first precipitated the strikes. The Spider had fought him once, permanently stiffened his ankle with a bullet. Did his presence here mean that the Brand was turning his attentions in that direction?

"All right, so you're Bosher," Wentworth rasped.

Bosher nodded. He had a broad, smiling face and small brilliant blue eyes that did not smile at all. "Yeah. I want to talk to you, Blinky."

Wentworth appeared to hesitate. He shoved his fists into his money-stuffed pockets, shrugged his shoulders and deliberately unbuttoned his coat so that it swung clear of an underarm gun.

"All right," he agreed ungraciously. "These two gees with you?" He scowled at the other two men, a nervous bouncy youth with jerky hands and a too-nice smile; another older and more deliberate man with the solemn look of a morgue attendant.

"We… met," Bosher said equably, as the three filed toward a corner table. "Blinky, this is the Undertaker; and this guy is the Jitterbug."

Wentworth allowed something of awe to show in Blinky McQuade's disguised face. Both men were killers. The Jitterbug had an ugly trick of hysterical laughter when he struck. It was loudest when his victims were slowest in dying. And the

Undertaker... deserved his name. Wentworth twisted his face into a dark scowl.

"I ain't afraid of nobody," he announced harshly. "Speak your piece. I got things to do."

Bosher seated them at his table, ordered drinks and did not speak until they were served. Wentworth was restless under the enforced delay. His minutes, the stingy little minutes in which he could be safe to work, were slipping past remorselessly. And the greater part of his task still lay ahead of him.

"Spit it out," he urged sharply. "I told you I got things to do."

"It's just possible," Bosher said calmly, "that we are going to do the same thing. If we are, say so. If not... you can go about your business. Believe it or not—" Bosher's voice changed subtly and Wentworth knew that he was repeating a formula. "Believe it or not, we are waiting for a phone call."

Wentworth hesitated. Was there a set answer to that formula, or would his mere recognition of it be enough? No way of telling, but as yet, no great danger attended failure to understand.

He narrowed his eyes behind the distorting lenses of the hooded glasses. "Funny," he mumbled. "Damned funny. I wasn't."

"No?" Bosher was purring, but Wentworth realized that he had not yet betrayed himself. "Then what were you waiting for?"

Wentworth snarled, "I came in here to listen to the radio. What do you think of that?"

IT WAS a stab in the dark, but it conformed with the facts that he had already detected. Bosher sat back with a relaxed air of satisfaction. "So," he murmured. "Now we understand each other. I have made a proposition to these two gentlemen. But perhaps you aren't interested?"

Blinky McQuade hunched a little farther over the table. His spatulate fingers were tense. "Look," he said slowly, and caution was bright in his voice. "Look, I ain't asked a thing, see? I ain't bad with a rod, but I ain't no expert like you other gees. Safe-cracking is what I like, and there ain't nobody can beat me at that. You know what I mean?"

Bosher was nodding, his face creased in its deep smile, his small eyes intent on Wentworth's disguised face. "Clear as a picture," he agreed.

For a while, they sat like that, four crooks in an Underworld hideout, calmly discussing murder by indirection. Wentworth was under no illusions as regards the plan of Jack Bosher. He seemed to be answering the Brand's summons only because he hoped to seize the weapon of the Brand, with these two lightning-swift killers to assist him. What he required from Blinky McQuade was that he should keep out of the fight that ensued… But it was strange that he should make his approach so openly. Apparently Bosher did not fear the Brand!

"Maybe it would be better I shouldn't go at all," Wentworth said slowly. "But I got paid, and there was going to be more."

Bosher nodded, and his hand slipped to his wallet in his inside pocket. Wentworth touched his tongue to his lips, and his hands were nervous.

"I can use a man like you… later," Bosher said as he fingered out bills. He folded them, slid two thousand dollars across the table, and Blinky McQuade seemed avid… Wentworth thought quietly that when this was over he would have a nice fat contribution for the trade farm he secretly financed to help boys who had slipped outside the law.

As he tucked the money into his pocket, Wentworth pushed up from the table. "Should I be here tomorrow night, maybe?" he said.

Bosher nodded, and Wentworth turned toward the door and, as the admiring Spike swung it open for him, he heard the rasping accents of a voice he knew break into the threnody of the radio, the voice of the Brand!

For an instant, Wentworth hesitated. He heard the Brand say, "The time is now. The place... *five... nine... twenty-four... one... s... r!*" It began to repeat, but Wentworth pushed brusquely out of the door and shuffled off into the shadows. Without doubt, each of those men had a code message of some sort. Either there were gaps which those numbers and letters would fill to make a completed message, or there were a number of words on a sheet of paper, and those numbers and letters indicated which ones were to be used to make up the complete message. It did not matter. Wentworth knew three men who would go together to the hideout of the Brand.

The Spider could find the way!

Wentworth glanced up at the white cold face of the Tower clock, and his breath hissed roughly over his teeth. Twenty minutes left before he must race to his seaplane and speed away to intercept Jackson, to deceive Chartres. Twenty minutes in which the Spider must follow this trail to its end and... remove the Brand!

Twenty minutes....

CHAPTER 7
THE BRAND'S MEN MEET!

THE WAREHOUSE was a squat black shadow against the wind-ruffled mirror of the river. Even to accustomed eyes, the place seemed sinister by contrast with the fashionable Riverbank Arms just beyond it, one of those lavish apartments built in the midst of slums. So it was not strange that taxis should rumble into the neighborhood, or that men should go there at night. No one watched as they disappeared, one by one, into the dark recesses of the warehouse. No one *seemed* to watch....

Going there alone, according to instructions, the Undertaker smiled his dour approval. It was pretty slick, pretty smooth. He would have to remember this for future use... When the taxi had sped on, he walked the short block to the warehouse and found the narrow door that had been described. For just a moment, he hesitated outside that door. Then he thrust his right hand into his overcoat pocket, felt his revolver... and went in.

At first, there was nothing to be seen; then he noticed a luminous arrow on the floor that pointed straight ahead. And after that another, and another. The Undertaker's smile stayed on his mouth, and he moved quietly forward along the indicated path, came presently to a small cubicle against the black wall of the warehouse. This time he did not hesitate, but stepped promptly through the door. As he closed it, harsh light slapped into his eyes, and his hand tightened about the gun.

A mocking voice whispered to him, "Welcome, Undertaker! You are prompt! And that is as the Brand likes it!"

The Undertaker's light-strained eyes peered about him and saw no one in the room at all. A loudspeaker, of course; the Brand was keeping himself out of sight. The Undertaker's face held its gravity, but there was hate and, perhaps, a touch of fear in the small blue eyes. If the Brand did not show himself at all, it would be hard for Bosher to pull off his coup!

"In the closet, Undertaker," came the voice again, "are robes and masks. You will put one on!"

The Undertaker moved stolidly toward the closet indicated by the unseen speaker, for it came to him sharply that he could be seen! There were red robes hanging on hooks in the closet, a dozen or so of them. On the floor were some things that looked like pinkish football helmets until he had one in his hands. Then he saw that it was steel, and made into the likeness of a face. It would cover his whole face, and there was a bald dome to cover his hair!

The Undertaker fought down a curse. What the hell was the use of all this mumbo-jumbo? Only amateurs always pulled stuff like this; they read it in magazines. Well, for the present he would follow orders—until Bosher came. He dropped the robe over his head, slid on the mask and looked about through the slits of the eyes. It was then he realized the purpose of the robes. With these and the masks, no man could be distinguished from his neighbor! Then how in hell would Bosher and the Jitterbug recognize him? How would he know when to strike? It was as if the Brand knew all about it in advance! The Undertaker felt cold....

He heard the voice rasping at him and obeyed without delay, entering a narrow elevator and allowing it to lift him to the second floor. He told himself grimly that maybe this amateur wasn't so dumb. This would have to be handled very carefully. The first step was to spot Bosher and the Jitterbug, and then....

The door of the elevator opened automatically, and he stepped out into a lavishly furnished conference room with a long table covered in green baize down its middle. There were three other men in crimson before him. They sat about the table, with their bodies curiously lengthened by the fact that the robes covered their arms also; their faces were of course hidden behind identical masks.

"In this room," rasped the omnipresent voice of the Brand, "there will be no speaking, except by myself. Understand? *The Bolt* is focused on you, and if one of you disobeys, *all of you die!*

"Sit down, number four!"

THE UNDERTAKER realized that the Brand meant *him*. His feet stumbled a little as he moved toward a chair, and something like panic made his black soul shiver with cold. Under the focus of the weapon that could squeeze out a man's brain! The Undertaker was glad the mask hid his face, glad that his trembling hands could not be seen. It looked like Bosher would have to postpone his attempt to seize the weapon. Well, let *him* worry! The Undertaker would do nothing without his word. He felt sudden laughter pump at his throat, and he strangled it fearfully. By God, what a joke on Blinky McQuade! The Brand had threatened the death of any man who failed to attend, and Blinky McQuade had taken a bribe to stay away! The Undertaker could scarcely contain his laughter. He didn't recognize it as the hysteria of fear....

The men came in slowly, one by one, and each wore the scarlet robe and the transfiguring mask. There were not even nervous hands visible to betray identity, though there was strong tension among the gathered men. The deadly cold repetition of the order of silence—the threat of the Bolt, which at any moment might wipe them all out of existence—beat upon their courage and shattered it. They were slaves who waited for a master, for these were men who lived by force and violence—and knew what those things could accomplish. They were men who had killed coldly, without feeling. They were men who might fight like cornered animals in a trap; or might throw down their guns and call quaveringly for quarter. But here, there was nothing to fight, there was no chance. Even the courage of cornered animals had deserted them. They were slaves who waited upon a cruel master....

But now, every chair about the table was taken, and twelve identical faces, steel masks actually, regarded each other across the green baize expanse.

Suddenly, the whisper of the Brand was all about them. It no longer seemed to have the mechanical rasp of a loudspeaker. The men about the table swayed a little. The Brand had entered the room! He was... one of them! Yet no head turned to regard a neighbor, and the whisper was thin and piercing and ugly.

"I have brought you here," came the slow, mocking voice,

"because you were too cowardly to recognize your own advantage. I need a few men to help me, and I have chosen you carefully. I know the abilities of each man, and shall know how to use them. In exchange, I shall make you wealthy beyond all your hopes. No one, nothing, can stand against *the Bolt!*

"It shall open vaults for us, shall blast down opposition. Untold wealth, my cowards, if you serve me well. If you fail… we shall see if your coward's flesh can withstand the force that crumples steel!"

Around the table, the men still sat like automatons. The whispering voice broke into a thin, senseless giggle that poured liquid ice down the spines of the men who were the prisoners of fear.

"For the present," said the Brand, "that will be all. When I need you, the command will come. *See to it that you obey!*"

The voice fell silent, but it was not the silence of dismissal. There was more to come. The feeling of it was there in the air, palpable as bare steel. When the figure at the foot of the table rose gravely, every head pivoted that way. With a sense of unreality, they saw that red robe part down the front, and the wings that were flung backward over the shoulders like a cape were sable black, were the color of the black eye of the heavy automatic that stared at them all!

In the same instant, the man who stood whipped off the steel mask that concealed face and head, and they were looking into a face they all knew, that they all feared! It was a lipless face, with a predatory beak of a nose, with gray-blue eyes that stabbed like individual steel bullets beneath a shock of lank black hair. And as they stared, the man's shoulders lost their square set and became hunched and twisted.

A cry that was a muted sigh of terror lifted from the assembled men. They voiced a single word:

"*The Spider!*"

IT WAS truly the Spider who crouched there at the foot of the table. He was not a large man, but his presence dominated the room as if he had been Colossus. His eyes battered through the steel masks.

"Take off your masks!" the Spider ordered. "There is not one of you who does not deserve death at my hands, but I am seeking only one man. If you do not resist, the rest shall survive. *Take off your masks!*"

The whisper of the Brand sighed through the room, and still there was no hint as to its source. "The first man who moves to take off his mask shall feel… *the Bolt!* You are beaten, Spider! Throw down your gun!"

Beneath the shaggy false brows of the Spider, Wentworth's eyes were lightning swift. He knew that the Brand could not release the Bolt on him alone, that other men must necessarily die with him. He knew also that, if the Bolt could be used, the Brand would not have waited to speak. But it would be impossible to convince the others of this fact.

Wentworth's left hand flew out to the man beside him. He seized the mask and ripped it upward and, at the far end of the table, he saw the flicker of a scarlet robe where a hand moved swiftly in concealment. The automatic in Wentworth's right hand jerked, and the slam of the shot crowded the long room with concussion. The man slammed back in his chair, wavered slowly and then crashed over backwards to the floor. The mask bounced from his skull, and Wentworth's lightning glance skimmed his face. He swore softly. A vicious killer....

He glanced toward his left, and saw that the other man he had unmasked was a lawyer whose specialty was blackmail. There were great beads of sweat on his forehead, and his face was gray.

Wentworth seized his chance instantly. "The Brand is dead!" he snapped. "All of you, off with those masks if you want to live!"

He hurled Bosher bodily—straight toward the other masked and robed figures...

Men's hands lifted fumblingly beneath the robes, and three masks were off before the Brand's voice hissed poisonously in the room.

"Spider, look out the window!" it said. "I expected you, and prepared for your reception. Look out the window, Spider. Take your time. No one will make an attempt upon you. You will surrender, of your own free will!"

Wentworth's glance rested briefly on the three more unmasked men. All criminals that he knew. And he did not believe any was the Brand. Scarcely clever enough. There were six others in the room who still wore their masks. Six more... and there were six bullets in the automatic! The muzzle quested hungrily. Fury was pumping through his veins. Every man he had uncovered deserved death a hundred times over. Better that they should die here and now than that the Brand should escape.

"Spider, look out the window, or it will be too late!"

But, damn it, suppose the Brand was not in the room? He had been sure the man was here, but now his confidence wavered. He must make sure, and then—But what could be this menace outside the window? No armed man with a leveled gun, he knew. His side glance had revealed that much. Slowly, Wentworth backed away from the foot of the table, so that he still commanded the seated men and yet could see the window. A block away was the rich apartment building, the Riverbank Arms, with its hundred apartments, its many scores of residents.

"Now, Spider," said the Brand softly, "you see why you must surrender at once, do you not? Perhaps I should explain. Do you notice anything peculiar about the apartment building, Spider?"

Wentworth's eyes came to sharp focus, and a great cry tore its way up into his throat—and died there. There were a few dark windows in the apartment, and over those played a ghostly blue-white brilliance. It sparked, too, from the wrought-iron railings of the terraces, stood up in small twisting flames from the supports of the marquee! No need to ask what caused those flames! The Brand had charged the entire building with his damnable machine. It was ready... ready to be smashed to bits, with all the hundreds of human lives it contained, by the terrific implosion which the Brand could loose!

"Well, Spider?" said the Brand softly. "Shall I discharge the Bolt—or will you drop your gun and surrender? You are the devout defender of the innocent, Spider; the paladin of the people. Here are about four hundred people, more or less, that you can save by simply dropping your gun. Well, Spider, will you drop the gun, or shall I discharge... *the Bolt?*"

BENEATH HIS makeup, the face of Richard Wentworth grew pale, as it would never do for fear of his own peril. The blue-white flames told him that the Brand told the absolute truth... and four hundred lives were at stake against his own! For a mad instant, Wentworth hesitated on the brink of hurling himself upon the remaining men about the table. His uncanny marksmanship might well eliminate all of them before a single one could release the Bolt, but suppose... suppose the Brand were not in the room!

Wentworth had one more desperate chance. If he dropped the gun, the Brand might then reveal himself. The Spider would be without a weapon, and there was not a man in the room who

121

did not have one. He thought that he could find a way to rid the world of the Brand!

"I'll give you five seconds more, Spider," the Brand said, and his gloating was plain in his voice. "Five seconds... and then the apartment collapses!"

Five seconds... Wentworth's mind flicked to the passage of time. His own quota of time was almost finished. At nine o'clock he would have to dash to the seaplane, or his carefully built alibi was destroyed... and Chartres would have another fragment of proof that he was the Spider! Wentworth's hand was entirely steady, his voice came out clearly.

"You win, for the present, Brand," he said. "I will drop my gun!"

Wentworth held out his gun at arm length, and allowed it to fall to the floor! Then he folded his arms. His eyes seemed steady and direct, but they saw every movement within the room. Let the Brand show himself now, let him but betray his identity by the slightest movement....

The Brand laughed softly. "You men who remain," he said mockingly, "pull the guns you were too cowardly to use before, and cover the Spider. Shoot, if he moves!"

Wentworth's heart began to beat harder as he saw the men draw their guns; all of them obeyed. The Brand might be among them, obeying his own orders; he might be outside the room... Wentworth watched narrowly, and knew that his life hung by a brace of seconds.

"Now, Jitterbug," came the Brand's voice. "Go over and knock the Spider over the head. Don't be too gentle, but don't kill him either!"

The Jitterbug removed his mask, and there was a happy smile on his face as he circled toward Wentworth's left side. Wentworth stood immovable, arms folded, a calm smile on his mouth. And still his eyes scanned the men before him, seeking any slightest clue that would betray the Brand to him. The Jitterbug was almost beside him. He had his heavy gun lifted to smash down on Wentworth's head! He laughed shrilly and the gun flashed down… Wentworth was not beneath it!

HIS FOLDED arms flashed upward, and his hands clamped about the Jitterbug's wrist. The impetus of the blow helped him, and he twirled the gunman forward, over his shoulder, and hurled him bodily straight toward the others! There was an eager crashing of guns, a death scream torn from the killer's lips… but Wentworth was leaping forward to the attack. In a moment, he had wrenched off the masks of two of the men and was leaping toward the others.

The masks were off and guns were swiveling toward him, but Wentworth had a second weapon in his hand now. Its muzzle roved to seek its victim—and an oath squeezed out between his thinned lips. All three were crooks whom he knew. *The Brand was not in the room!*

"Enough, Spider," came the Brand's mocking voice. But the whisper seemed closer. "I have given you too much leeway already. Will you surrender… or shall four hundred people die that you may live? The discharge is ready, the building is primed… I need only send *the Bolt*. A last time, Spider!"

123

Guns ringed the Spider in, but it was not of those that he was thinking. Four hundred people… and without a doubt the Brand would carry out his threat to destroy the building. Weighed against that, the Spider's life was unimportant.

Wentworth realized that it was not his life alone that was at stake; the honor and the reputation of Richard Wentworth, disclosed finally in death as the Spider, would suffer also. Nita might well be prosecuted, Ram Singh, Jackson… for it was drawing very close to nine o'clock, the ultimate limit of his alibi built up with Chartres. His non-appearance and Chartres' discovery of the deception might not be final proof, but if the Spider were dead, it would be evidence enough. Yes, not only his own life was a stake, but also the future of all whom he held dear.

Very clearly, Wentworth saw these things. But these were only four lives… and in the building there were four hundred other human beings with an equal right to life, to happiness. The scales tipped….

Wentworth straightened slowly, and his gray-blue eyes were grim. Deliberately, he tossed his gun to the floor; his last gun. And he stood waiting.

"Shoot him in the left leg, Undertaker!" the Brand ordered.

Before the words were finished, a gun stabbed through the red robe of one of the men, and Wentworth felt the lead hammer against his leg. He was hurled backward, but managed to remain erect. He braced his shoulders against the wall and held his head up. There was still challenge in his eyes.

The Brand giggled. "We must take these little precautions,

Spider," he said. "Thank you for your surrender! It will assist me immeasurably in my... work!"

The distant clear notes of a bell began to shiver through the night. Fighting the agony of his wound, holding himself stiffly while the killers closed in about him like wolves about a wounded stag, Wentworth counted the strokes deliberately. Ah, yes, nine o'clock... Now his alibi was gone. God help Nita, and the city's thousands, now. Ah, Nita....

CHAPTER 8
DEATH TO THE SPIDER!

IT WAS exactly at nine o'clock when Nita, driven by an anxiety that she could not quell, turned sharply to the telephone and dialed Richard Wentworth's home. The bell buzzed on and on into silence. Nita tried to tell herself that this was nothing unusual, but she knew that it was. Never had she known Dick to leave his home entirely empty. For a while, she was on the verge of going to his apartment, but she calmed herself with an effort. After all, she had no reason to believe that Dick was in any special danger now.

Nita found herself standing by the broad windows that looked out over the black reaches of the Hudson, but the scene scarcely registered on her mind. Her thoughts were all turned inward. She forced herself to face calmly the waiting emptiness that had filled so much of her life in latter years. She sat in a deep chair by the window, her eyes staring blankly ahead of her. In her lap, her white slender hands twisted and twisted....

She was still there in that chair, still staring widely when the rising sun stretched the shadow of the building out toward the river and flashed red on the windshields of passing cars. So profound was her self-compelled lethargy that when, some while later, the phone bell trilled, her head turned only slowly toward the instrument. Through a long instant, she still stared at it—then she bounded to her feet with a wild start and snatched it up. Her throat closed against her words, but when finally she could speak, the sound of her voice was clear and even.

"Nita van Sloan speaking… Oh, Jackson!" Nita was silent then through a long while, listening to swift words, the story of Wentworth's planned alibi, and his failure to arrive. "I got away from Chartres before he could find out about me posing as the major, Miss Nita," Jackson rushed on. "Three times I lost him and doubled back to the meeting place, but the major never showed up. And finally Chartres started shooting. It's taken me until just now to lose him. Not much question he'll order our arrest, but I wanted to report first. There's no word of the major on the air, or in the newspapers."

Nita knew a violent throbbing of her heart, knew the certainty of disaster, but she compelled her voice to remain calm. These were brave warriors, these comrades of Dick, but they looked to her for leadership as naturally as they turned to Dick. She must not fail them now.

"Have you checked on the seaplane?" she asked. "He might have made a forced landing… Never mind, I'll do so myself. It will be better if you and Ram Singh stay right there. If Chartres comes for you, you will insist that it was the major in the car.

Naturally, you don't know why he did as he did—if he did it! Call the major's lawyers and tell them you're threatened with arrest, and to prepare for *habeas corpus* action. I'll phone further orders."

Nita swung away from the phone, and her movements were efficient. Her mind was working with clarity, though her heart seemed to swell to suffocation. If Dick's airplane had not been taken from its ramp, there remained only one explanation of his absence: a disaster of some sort. She would not permit her mind to go beyond that thought.

FIVE MINUTES later, she was driving her fast coupé across the city toward the pier where Wentworth maintained his seaplane. As she neared it, she heard the motor explode into life, heard its warm throbbing, and joy leaped to her brain. But when she jumped from the car and ran to where she could see the ship, she knew the sharp stab of disappointment. The man in the greasy cap was only a mechanic. She swung toward the manager of the pier, who was coming toward her anxiously.

"We've kept the motor warmed up all night, according to orders, Miss van Sloan," he reported, "but Mr. Wentworth never showed up at all. Do you think there's any use in keeping it up?"

Nita said, slowly, "No, no use at all. He apparently... changed his plans."

She turned toward the door, heard soft strains of music from a radio set in the small office near the street entrance. The music broke off.

"We interrupt this program," came the sweetly inflected voice of the announcer, "to bring you a news bulletin from New York. Another of those strange explosions that have terrified the city in the last forty-eight hours occurred this morning at the main office of the Gotham Trust Bank. An undetermined number of persons were killed. Police estimate that at least five were in the offices at the time. The police also report that there is no doubt that the crime was committed by the man who calls himself the Brand. The thieves wore red robes and curious steel masks which concealed their entire heads.

"And here's another bulletin that was just handed to me!

"The police report that the Spider assisted the Brand in this robbery! He was seen to shoot down at least one policeman, and the surviving officers insist that they wounded the Spider! However, the men in red robes carried him off with them.

"That is all for the present. We will be back with further last minute news later on. Don't forget to keep tuned to this station…."

The words blurred in Nita's mind. She was already striding rapidly toward her car. News of Dick at last… but such news! She flung herself behind the wheel of the coupé, whipped it in a tight turn. But, actually, she had heard nothing about Dick at all! The broadcast had stated the Spider shot a policeman! That was a thing that Dick would never do, even to save his own life! Then it was a *false* Spider who paraded in the robes of Richard Wentworth!

Nita drove a daring course through the morning traffic. She was unaware of the brilliant clarity of the morning, of the pale yellow sunlight that slanted into narrow streets. Her eyes stared wide; her thoughts were like knives twisted slowly in her heart.

If the Brand dared to clothe a man in the Spider's robes, it meant one of two things: either the Spider was his prisoner, or the Spider... was dead!

She peered about her uncertainly and saw that she was only a block from police headquarters. Plainly, that was where she had intended to go. She realized that now, and her full lips tightened with resolution. Kirkpatrick must know that it could not actually be the Spider who had done these things! He must change the reports at once, and....

The hoarse whine of a siren cut in on her thoughts. Nita braked sharply, just short of the corner, and an instant later the limousine of Stanley Kirkpatrick flashed past! Nita glimpsed the commissioner's rugged profile as he leaned tensely forward in the rear. She saw the dapper, slight figure of Raoul Chartres beside him. Nita hurled her coupé forward in the wake of the racing police car!

NITA DID not reason the thing she did, but as she tooled grimly after the powerful limousine, she understood. If Kirkpatrick was racing out on an emergency call, it must concern one of two things... The Brand, or... *the Spider!*

Nita's hand dropped to the holster affixed to the front of the seat and extracted the thirty-two automatic which Dick had taught her to use almost as expertly as he could. Nita would never love firearms. They had brought too much sorrow into her life. But she felt a satisfaction in the weight of the weapon in her competent small hand, and she was utterly confident of her ability to use it, if the need arose. She slipped it into the pocket of her sport coat.

Abruptly, Nita stiffened at the wheel of the car. A new sound

129

smote her ears—the racketing of gunfire close at hand! She was braking when the big limousine whipped around a corner to the left; she managed to make the turn also. She was a half-block behind the commissioner's car, and now she saw a dozen blue-uniformed policemen crouched in doorways, concentrating their fire on the front of a massive bank building near the next corner.

For the moment that was all she saw, and then a stream of scarlet gushed from the doors of the bank! They were the red-robed men of the Brand! For that one instant, she saw them, and then all her attention, all her heart, concentrated on one figure that stood out sharply against that crimson background. It was a man clothed in a black cape, with a wide-brimmed black hat upon his head. His shoulders were twisted hideously, and in his hands he gripped a short, blunt stick like a cane. Even as she stared, blue-white flame streaked from the end of that cane, and two policemen slammed violently together. Their bodies flattened in a grotesque embrace, and then they lay together in a shattered heap of flesh and masonry.

Stunned at the sight, Nita checked herself in the act of climbing from the coupé. Her automatic was in her fist, but she had forgotten it, forgotten everything except the horror of the thing she had seen. This, she realized, was the Bolt! And it had been fired by the Spider! For that sickening instant, Nita knew a mounting horror. Then she shook her head, drove herself to the pavement. Of course, it wasn't the Spider! But she was still shaken. If *she* felt that instant of doubt, she could scarcely blame the police verdict!

Nita lifted her automatic and sent lead whining toward the red ranks. She saw one of the men, carrying a sack across his shoulder, stagger under the impact of lead. She swung the muzzle toward the figure in black, took deliberate aim… Abruptly, she let the gun sag. She knew it was not the Spider. She knew it. But she could not bring herself to fire!

Ahead of her, she heard Kirkpatrick's crisp voice bell out: "Get the Spider!" he shouted. "All of you, aim at the Spider! Bring him down first!"

A cry of protest rose in Nita's throat. She saw Kirkpatrick poise deliberately, his long-barreled revolver lifted, and she knew how terribly accurate he could be. She started forward… and saw that horrible blunt cane in the hands of the man in black swing toward Kirkpatrick!

The shot from Kirkpatrick's revolver, the flicker of blue flame from the cane—came at the same instant! The man in the Spider's robes doubled up suddenly. Nita had seen men die like that from a heart shot. Shock and despair swept her, and then she felt herself jerked from her feet and flung forward! Falling to the pavement, she caught herself instinctively, and so she did not see the thing that happened.

LABORIOUSLY, SHE dragged her body from the pavement. She understood then. It had been the implosion of the Bolt that had yanked her off her feet. Only the fact that she had been at a considerable distance from the point where it took effect had saved her. It had struck Kirkpatrick's car, and where the powerful limousine had stood, there was a jumble of wreckage. The welded steel body was crumpled as if a giant fist had squeezed it together.

Kirkpatrick was flat on the sidewalk, just beginning to stir. He had been flattened also, but fortunately the Bolt had missed him. Nita's eyes flashed beyond him toward the spot where the man who wielded the Bolt had fallen. There were two of the red-robed men beside him. As she watched, they yanked him up and raced toward a waiting car. In the same instant, it was streaking away!

Nita whirled back to her coupé, flung it violently forward to where Kirkpatrick was staggering to his feet.

"Here, Stanley!" she called. "Your car is smashed!"

Kirkpatrick's head turned heavily. He surveyed the street. Five of his men were stretched upon the pavement, and the last of the Brand's cars was streaking around the far corner.

"After them!" Kirkpatrick cried hoarsely. "After them!"

In two long strides, he reached Nita's car. Instantly, she had the coupé racing forward again. Her doubts were all resolved, and a fierce anger had taken the place of her fears. She wanted now to overtake that man who dared to masquerade in the Spider's robes. It had been only the shock of seeing that familiar figure that had shaken her for the moment.

"You killed that impostor in the Spider's robes," she said coolly. "It was a heart shot."

Her hands were tight upon the wheel, and her eyes were keen for the tangle of traffic. As she passed, a police car spurted forward, took the corner a split-second ahead of her, but she managed the turn expertly.

Kirkpatrick pulled his eyes away from the chase. "I didn't realize it was you, Nita," he said heavily. "What are you doing here?"

Nita explained she had been on her way to see him when she saw his car. "I wanted to tell you that, even on the basis of the news reports, it is apparent that this man is not the Spider," she said. "He shot a policeman. That is something the Spider would never do!"

Kirkpatrick's lips closed thinly, and he made no direct response. "Where is Dick?" he asked.

Nita felt her heart contract at the cold implacability of Kirkpatrick's voice. "I thought he was with you," she said, and tried to make it sound like surprise.

Kirkpatrick did not speak. Nita tried to carry on the pretense, and could not. She concentrated on driving. The siren of the police coupé ahead was tearing a hole through the traffic in the wake of the fleeing killers. Suddenly, the police car was a blaze of blue light. Nita swerved wildly, cocked a wheel over the curb, and passed the suddenly arrested machine. She had a glimpse of it—a crumpled mass of wreckage. Pallor crept across her cheeks, but she did not slacken speed. Kirkpatrick had his long-barreled revolver in his hand and was thrusting the upper half of his body out the window on the right. She tried to hold very steadily on her course. The black butt of the Bolt was just visible in the back window of the car she followed. Her hands tightened on the wheel. She heard Kirkpatrick's gun crash. At the same instant, she swerved wildly to the right, fighting to straighten out again. THE CAR wavered, and was sucked sideways bodily. She was momentarily blinded by the flicker of blue-white flame...

but it had missed. And she saw that Kirkpatrick had not! The crooks' car was in a frantic skid. It straightened, bucked wildly, and took a corner on two screaming tires. It flicked out of sight and, an instant later, there was a tearing crash!

"After them!" Kirkpatrick ordered grimly.

Nita hit the corner at full speed, slammed on the brakes and wrenched over the wheel. The tires shrieked in furious complaint. The coupé heeled far over, but the rear end came around. She ground the accelerator to the floor. Through a frantic instant, the coupé continued its mad skid, then the tires took hold and hurled the machine forward. She had a flashing glimpse of men in scarlet scrambling out of the crumpled machine. Guns blazed in their fists. A man with the Bolt gripped in both fists, sprang clear and braced himself to level the weapon!

Kirkpatrick's revolver blasted, and Nita knew achingly that he had missed. The coupé was traveling with furious speed, but it would not be fast enough to dodge… a bolt of lightning! Nita's teeth set fiercely. These were the men who had seized Dick, who were blackening his name. These were the men who were killing people in the city streets with this weapon of horror. There was just one chance, a slim and desperate one. But even as the thought flashed across Nita's mind, she put her plan in action.

She drove the car at top speed straight at the crouching man!

For a sharp instant, the man stood firm, lifting the Bolt to destroy them. Then his courage broke and he whirled to leap aside! Nita tried, in that split-second, to swerve also. She had achieved her purpose, and she sickened at the thought of the death she might inflict. It was too late. The right front side of the car caught the man in the red robe in mid-leap. A quivering jar ran through the coupé, and the man in the red robe... *flew!* Like a hard-driven ball, his body flew through the air. There was a despairing shriek on his lips. His arms flung wide, as if the thin air might offer him a handhold upon life. When he struck, it was against the steel base of a lamppost. His body... wrapped around it!

Whether it was the shock, or the aftermath of that wild skidding turn, Nita lost control of the coupé. She was standing on the brake, fighting the wheel at the instant of impact, and the car whined in a skidding turn, straightened, whipped the other way. It caromed from the side of a parked car, turned broadside and charged straight across the street. Nita was still fighting to halt her juggernaut when it bounced high over the curb and slammed its nose through a plate-glass window. It trundled its entire length into the shop and came to a halt.

Dizzily, Nita thrust herself back from the wheel over which she had been tossed. She turned toward Kirkpatrick. He was slumped forward, head against the shatterproof windshield, which radiated myriad fractures. He was out cold. Nita tried to climb from behind the wheel. She groped at her pocket for the automatic... and the world went black around her. A sigh pushed out between her lips as she slumped, unconscious, beside Kirkpatrick. Perhaps, was her waning thought, she had done a little to help convince Stanley Kirkpatrick of his error; had done a little something for Dick....

THE ROOM in which Wentworth was imprisoned was a narrow cell beneath the surface of the earth. No effort had been made to bind him. Yet he never touched a wall; he kept a good distance always between himself and the flimsy door with the peephole through which now and again the Brand's steel mask peered in upon him. And there was good reason for his restraint.

Always, over the door and the walls, there played the faint flickering blue-white flame of electricity! Wentworth had been warned that if he so much as touched one of those barriers, he would discharge the Bolt! The walls of his room would fold in upon him!

For the most part, Wentworth lay motionless upon the cot that had been provided for him. His leg wound gave him continuous pain, but he thought that it would mend without complications. Once a day, the peephole opened in the door and the Brand peered in, to mock him with his thin giggle and bitter words. Every day, also, he thrust in newspapers which told of the ceaseless raids of the Brand's men, assisted by the Spider! Wentworth had himself completely under control, but his keen brain for once could figure no escape from the trap into which he had been flung. He knew too little about the operation of the Bolt to be able to circumvent the power which would destroy him. Even that he would have risked, if he could have been sure of destroying also this beast who mocked him, and of wiping from the earth the murderous weapon that the man used.

So the Brand mocked him, and boasted of his next exploit— and on the following day presented the newspapers which proved that he had fulfilled his plans in detail. Wentworth began to rage at the Brand. He flew into fury at sight of the newspapers which proved the claims of the man; at the fact that the police had promulgated a "shoot-to-kill" order against the Spider.

"It is a curious thing," the Brand whispered through the peephole, "but the police seem to have a particular hatred for the Spider. I have had four men killed in the robes of the Spider, and two of them the Commissioner himself killed!"

Wentworth knotted his fists, and his face was twisted in anger. "You're driving me mad with this stuff," he shouted hoarsely. "Keep your confounded newspapers out of here! Keep your devil's face away from that peephole!"

The Brand giggled. "So the news annoys you, Spider?"

Wentworth was panting, apparently in the effort at control. Actually, behind that mask of rage, his brain was cool and calculating. At last, he had formed a plan. It might not succeed in freeing him, but perhaps he could warn the world of what impended, and thus thwart this mad genius of murder!

"I can take all you give me." Wentworth spat out the words between his teeth. "After all, you can spare only a few minutes a day to torture me, and I have the rest of the time to recover! And I don't have to read the newspapers, you know. I have willpower enough left not to read them!"

The Brand was glaring at him with shallow hateful eyes. "Is that true now?" he asked softly. "You give me an idea!"

Wentworth took a slow step forward, then checked himself as the flames crackled more loudly over the surface of the door.

"Yes, indeed," said the Brand, "you give me an idea. I think I know one thing you couldn't resist; something that would be with you more than a few minutes a day!"

Wentworth retreated, and terror twisted his face. "Don't do it!" he cried. "Damn you, don't do it! Don't you put a radio in here! Look, Brand, you don't want to drive me mad. I might even be some help to you someday. But if you destroy my mind—"

The peephole clicked shut, and Wentworth shouted curses against the closed door, but there was elation in his breast. If only he could persuade the Brand to put a radio receiver in his cell, he thought that he might yet defeat the killer! But so many days had passed; so many human beings had suffered under the slashing attack of the Bolt!

Yet, just let him get that radio set in his cell....

THE DAYS that had passed had not been kind to Nita. There had been no injury to her in the crackup of her car, but the shock of collision had prevented her making a foray before the men of the Brand had fled—and carried the false Spider with them.

She had pleaded with Kirkpatrick to believe her theory about this new Spider who killed the police, or any other human being who blocked his evil intentions. Finally, Kirkpatrick had refused to admit her to his office, or to his home! Jackson and Ram Singh were awaiting trial on charges of conspiracy to obstruct the law, and she had been unable to have them released on bail. She knew that she owed her own freedom more to the lucky accident of helping the police than to any other thing. They would have found it difficult to make out a case against her under the circumstances.

Bitterly, Nita came to a decision. There was only one way for her to end this condemnation of the Spider, one way for her to find once and for all the solution of the mystery that surrounded

Dick's disappearance. She must herself identify and capture the Brand! There was no other solution!

It was a grim responsibility for Nita to assume, and there was nothing at all to point toward the person who might be responsible for the crimes. Thanks to the power of the Bolt, the red-robed men had never left behind them one of their number; never failed to carry out their objectives. The marvel of it was that always they seemed to know just when to strike, just when the banks would carry the maximum of cash. The police talked of inside information, but Nita knew that there were other methods than that of learning the status of banks. She spent long hours digging through the bank statements and treasury reports. And she found the information she sought: the bank which, according to clearing-house records, should have on hand the largest amount of deposits....

That same night, she went to a public phone and put through a call to Kirkpatrick on his private wire. When she heard the receiver lifted at the other end of the wire, she laughed—and over the wire went the thin, mocking laughter of the Spider!

Nita kept her voice in a harsh whisper. That way, she knew, if she were skillful, Kirkpatrick could not tell that it was a woman who spoke.

"Ah, Kirkpatrick," she whispered in the Spider's mocking vein. "It is scarcely flattering to me that you mistake that impostor for the Spider. No, do not speak, for I shall talk only for fifteen seconds. Listen carefully! Tomorrow, the Brand will rob the Ameredo Trust! I expect you will be there to take care of the matter!"

Nita laughed again and hurried from the phone booth. She was barely two blocks away in her coupé when she heard the raging of the police sirens soaring into the district. She had made it by only a narrow margin!

ONCE MORE at home, she set diligently to work and, when dawn came, she was ready. The disguise was complete… When the Brand struck, there would be a new Spider there to meet him, a Spider who fought on the side of justice, as always!

Nita got to her feet and moved to the window. As on that other dread day when first she had received the intelligence of Dick Wentworth's disappearance, the first red rays of the sun were fingering the river. Each dawn she had hoped vainly for some hint of Dick's fate, and there had been no slightest clue. This was the last desperate chance she faced today. She must take the field against an enemy who had triumphed over the police, who had overcome even the Spider—and she must take the field alone!

Nita knew her lowest hour of despair while the day brightened about her. Then slowly, her head came up and the line of her round determined chin was firm. If she failed, it would be gloriously. No dishonor would come to the Spider's robes through her! But she did not intend to fail! Dick's ultimate safety rested in her hands; and if she were too late for that, then… vengeance!

There was something close to reverence in the tender touch of her hands as she folded away the cape and placed it, with a broad-brimmed hat, and a steel face-mask, in a light satchel. She added a pound can of ether; it was her hope to take a prisoner and she could not count too much on her strength to strike a knockout blow.

Quickly then, she clothed herself in a dark mannish lounge suit with fitted trousers; pulled on a soft felt hat. There was grimmer preparation for the battle beneath that modish coat. Strapped to her shoulders was a pair of clip holsters, and the guns that rested in them were no longer the light tools of death to which she was most accustomed. They were duplicates of the heavy forty-five caliber automatics that the Spider loved!

She was painfully conscious of them as she picked up the satchel and made a last swift survey of the apartment. She recognized the fatalism behind that glance and fought against a feeling of failure, of despair. It was no wonder that she should feel misgivings, since she went alone against such odds! But she was the Spider's mate... Nita van Sloan forced a smile to her lips. Her chin lifted. Her step was brisk as she went out the door....

CHAPTER 9
ANOTHER SPIDER WALKS!

THE AMEREDO Trust lifted a white massive front in a business district of the crowded East Side. A row of one-story shops shouldered the bank on one side; across the street were tenement buildings, each with its iron fire escapes. The stores were just opening, but already children romped on the sidewalks, and dodged through the traffic.

A red truck jerked to a sudden halt before the Ameredo Trust. The driver climbed casually to the ground and ambled to the rear to swing open the double loading doors. At the same instant, the alarm bell on the side of the bank set up a wild clamor and, within the building, guns went mad!

For an instant the traffic stalled in the street, and then cars began to shoot madly forward, racing to escape the danger zone. Children stood transfixed on the pavement, and women, leaning stout arms on window sills, suddenly were wailing frantically the names of their children. The whole street went mad.

Then, louder than the shrieks of the women, came the sudden turbulence of police sirens. From side-street garages, the radio cars coursed toward the main avenue, and the officers were grimly ready, with weapons in their fists. They hit the avenue— and the doors of the bank whipped open to vomit the Brand's red-robed killers!

Each gripped a gun, and their lead scorched through the crowds. A woman slumped suddenly forward across her window sill, and hung there with arms dangling. Her weight shifted slowly forward. Beneath her, a child stared up with frightened eyes and screamed her name. She plunged head-foremost, in morbid answer to her child.

A truck driver, peering wildly toward the bank, took a bullet through the shoulder and was slammed across his cab. His pain-spasmed legs kicked, and the motor roared in fury. The truck crashed into two other cars before the litter beneath the wheels dragged it to a halt… A policeman, leaping from a radio car, sat down with a slug in the belly. He tried futilely to lift his revolver.

That was the scene when a man in the Spider's black robes leaped from the open doors of the truck. There was the same club-like stick in his fists, the Bolt. He took his stand deliberately, while the men in crimson streamed toward the escape truck. His eyes quested over the street, seeking out the police. The Bolt lifted and… across the street sounded the thin mockery of the Spider's awful laughter!

There was a wildness in that laughter which was strange to hear, and its shrillness ate like a knife into the brains of the men in red. They seemed suddenly frightened. Beside them stood a man in the Spider's robes, ready to fight their battles for them, but it was not from his lips that the laughter sounded.

Their eyes quested frantically, and then they saw… the *other* Spider!

Atop the one-story shop beside the bank stood a figure in black. There was no slouch to those narrow shoulders from which the cape billowed magnificently on the morning wind. The black hat was jaunty on a head that seemed curiously large for that slender body. The guns, too, were enormous. They were lifted high above the figure's head, outlined against the blue of the sky.

For just that instant, this diminutive, laughing Spider stood against the sky, while the guns of the Brand's men swung that way; while the weapons of the police dropped into line! Then, once more, hell blazed in the street.

ON THE roof, Nita van Sloan was conscious of the concentration of the guns on her person. Her flesh quivered, but she stood firm through that long moment, while her eyes, keen through the slits of her steel mask, searched the crouching ranks below. She stared at the man who dishonored the robes of the

Spider, and a small smile trembled on her lips. It was not Dick. She could never be deceived in that. No, not Dick. For the Bolt was swinging into line toward her, its blunt end gaping at her silhouetted figure.

The guns blasted, and Nita leaped far aside. She seemed too late, but she had been taught timing by the Master of Men himself! As Nita leaped, the heavy guns kicked against her slim hands! In the street, a man screamed! The man who defiled the robes of the Spider was hammered to the pavement by the double impact of Nita's lead! Nita tried to laugh again, but there was a sob in her voice. This was not a woman's work she performed! But the thought of Dick buoyed her spirits. There was no love of death in Wentworth's heart either; he, too, had moments of black depression from which even her sympathy scarcely served to lift him. She was fighting for Dick now!

Nita repeated that name each time the heavy guns bucked against her wrists, each time her bullets found a target below.

The air about her was alive with the shriek of lead. Nita moved as Dick had taught her, a long leap, and a short one, a dodge and a crouch; never in the same spot for two successive seconds. And always, the guns in her hands blasted their fury into the street below. Two more of the red-robed killers were down beside the

NITA VAN SLOAN

tail of the truck. Nita's lead searched through the hood of the car, and presently black smoke spurted from beneath it, followed by tongues of flame!

Then, from the interior of the truck, a man plunged with a submachine gun in his fists! He pivoted, flung up the muzzle. Nita snapped her right gun into line, and heard it click emptily! Frantically she hurled herself aside, and the first spray of lead missed. She whipped over her left-hand gun. There was scarcely time to aim, and her wrists were aching with the weight of the weapons, with the leashed fury of the recoil. She squeezed off the shot, and the man's head seemed to leap into space! For an instant, Nita was frozen there, motionless with horror. Then she saw that she had knocked off the man's steel mask! He was recovering from the blow, lifting the machine gun again—and Nita stared down into his exposed face.

A low cry started from Nita's lips, for she knew that face! It was sombre and lugubrious, save for the slitted eyes, and it had stared up at her once before from Dick's private Rogues' Gallery. This was the killer known as the Undertaker! Almost, that pause cost Nita her life. She stood transfixed. The machine-gun muzzle lifted, and Nita's left-hand gun also clicked empty!

Nita used the last trick she had then, kicking her feet out from under her, plummeting toward the roof. Her cape fluttered in the air behind her. It whipped and jerked like a living thing, and there, not a foot above her falling body, it was torn to shreds by the deluge of lead from below! But Nita was safe. She rolled swiftly across the surface of the roof, until the edge protected her. There was a sob in her throat as she surged to her feet and began desperately to race toward the rear.

HER SLENDER hands were trembling as she holstered one of the automatics and fumbled a clip into the base of the other. She stopped at the rear of the roof, and there seemed scarcely strength in her arms to force back the carriage and jack the first cartridge into the chamber. But it was done. A flying leap took her to the roof of a low shed; another, to the alleyway behind the bank building. Her car was close, and that was very fortunate. Nita staggered as she ran. Her brain was clear, but her body seemed to have absorbed the shock of the horror she had helped to create.

In the street beyond the buildings, guns lifted their voices in a high chant of fury as police and killers fought it out. But they were on equal terms now. The Bolt had been silenced by Nita's first shots, and the false Spider had fallen, too. She had struck a blow for Dick this day; she hoped she had helped break the power of the Brand. Fumblingly, as she ran, Nita tugged at the cape about her shoulders, finally whipped it free. She folded it into a bundle, peered into the street where her car was parked. People were fleeing in terror along that way. She would not be noticed.

She stripped off the steel mask, and bolted toward her car. Her breath was coming more easily now. A swift dash would take her from the danger zone, and she had acquired valuable information. She had identified one of the Brand's men, and she knew his associates. There was one named Jack Bosher, who was said to employ the Undertaker as a killer. If she could find Bosher... she might even find the Brand! A tremor seized Nita as she flung behind the wheel and kicked the motor to life.

She stuffed the mask and cape into the satchel. The can of ether tumbled out on the floor, and as she recovered it, she caught a glimpse of the street behind her in the rear-vision mirror. Two men in police blue were racing toward her, with their guns ready! Fiercely, Nita wrenched the coupé from the curb and tromped on the accelerator. One of the policemen stopped and took deliberate aim across his arm. Nita swerved wildly, and the lead smacked through the window behind her, tore through the cloth that lined the roof. Another bullet clanged into the metal of the car behind her, and then she whipped about the corner and was speeding northward.

WORRY DREW Nita's lovely brows together. It had been madness to use her own car for this affray. Dick would never have made such a foolish mistake. If they had spotted her license number… Nita shook her head. No time to worry about that now. She had to find out where Bosher was hiding himself these days, if indeed he bothered, and then… the ether can. Nita's lips set firmly together. She had dared to wear the Spider's robes, and she had succeeded. This much more, she would dare for Dick!

Abruptly, a car slammed out of the side street just ahead, and a cry leaped to Nita's lips. Her foot jammed down on the brake, but the car made no effort to avoid a collision. Instead, the chauffeur was deliberately braking, jerking the car about toward her! In that split second, Nita realized that the man was a police driver, and that the narrow, mocking face that peered at her from the tonneau was that of Raoul Chartres!

So much Nita saw before her coupé slammed against the side of the heavy limousine, wrenched sideways and was stalled, locked immovably against a lamp post. Nita's thought flew to the satchel at her side, the bullet holes in the cape and in the back window. She was trapped; she would be identified. But they would not believe her the genuine Spider. This would be another bit of evidence against Dick! Nita had been flung forward over the wheel by the force of the impact, and she hung that way limply. Her mind flashed to the guns beneath her arms. If more proof were needed, it would be found there, in matching those guns with the bullets in the men she had shot!

A terrible clarity had gripped Nita's mind, and though she remained slumped over the wheel, she was furiously planning. Her hands snapped to the guns beneath her arms and she dropped one to the floor, spilled the satchel atop them. There was no tremor at all now in her movements. Swiftly, she unscrewed the can of ether and allowed its contents to spill over the garments. The hot, sweet odor of it struck her nostrils, and she held her breath dizzily.

She heard a hand slap against the door beside her, wrenching it open. Nita thrust the muzzle of the remaining gun hard against the can of ether and pulled the trigger! Hands were closing on her left arm, even as she fired. She did not know whether it was the flaming blast that followed, or the grip of those hands that yanked her clear. She felt the heat sweep over her terribly, heard a man's hoarse shouted curse… and then she was lying in the street, looking at the blazing inferno of her coupé. A small smile moved Nita's lips, and she closed her eyes.

CHARTRES STOOD staring down at Nita where she lay upon the pavement, and there was a curious speculation in his eyes. The car was beyond reclamation, and whatever evidence was within it was destroyed also. The huge sacrifices that women would make for love were no new thing to him, but this was a matter which puzzled him greatly. He had no doubt that it had been Nita van Sloan herself who had fired from the roof of the building, who had shot down the man in the black robes upon the street. It proved at least that she did not believe the man was the Spider, and since she was willing thus to risk the horror of death by fire to save evidence against him….

Chartres shook his head slowly. Those two prisoners, who were servants of Wentworth; they, too, kept their lips resolutely closed. They laughed at threats, and no amount of questioning disturbed them at all. It had never been Chartres' experience that thieves held together so inexorably, or were so well served. This man Wentworth had… something. He remembered Kirkpatrick's reference to a patriotism of humanity, and a smile came into Chartres' eyes, a smile and a skeptical light. Nonsense. Wentworth might be well served, but he must profit somehow from these battles of his. In such matters, Raoul Chartres was a realist.…

He looked up as Kirkpatrick came striding forward, to stand and stare down also at the prostrate Nita. Kirkpatrick's lips squeezed together thinly.

"Is she hurt?" he demanded harshly.

Chartres shook his head slowly. "No—but it's not her fault that she isn't," he murmured. "She blew up her own car after the collision. A most resolute woman. Most resolute indeed!"

Kirkpatrick's sharp eyes seemed strangely relieved, and there was almost mockery in the smile that he masked by knuckling his mustache. "Then there is no proof that she was the Spider on the roof, who served us so well today."

Chartres shrugged slightly. "No proof, but there is a certainty. If you were to place her in the same position again, in the same clothing, I am certain that a score of people would identify her."

"No doubt," Kirkpatrick agreed dryly. "Or yourself either, were you to appear similarly. Come, we will take her to headquarters." He stooped over Nita, and his hands were gentle as he lifted her easily and went striding toward his limousine. Chartres followed, with his mincing short stride. His lemon-colored gloves were slightly smudged, and he looked down at them with disapproval. He flung himself irritably into the rear, where Nita was beginning to stir under Kirkpatrick's ministrations.

"I do not understand this thing at all," he snapped. "I have never known such loyalty among crooks and thieves."

For an instant, Kirkpatrick's eyes flashed angrily. Then he shrugged and continued to work over Nita.

"You do not answer, *M'sieur* Kirkpatrick?" Chartres said insistently. "Eh?"

Kirkpatrick said shortly, "We have discussed the matter at great length. I have no desire to repeat it."

"You believe then in the patriotism of this Spider," Chartres persisted, "and yet you hunt him. You order him shot on sight! It is a thing I do not understand."

Kirkpatrick's cheekbones had a high flush. "The Spider violates the law!" he said sharply. "It is not my business to weigh a man's motives. That is the prerogative of the courts. It is my task to enforce the law, and I should do it to the utmost of my ability, if the violator were my own brother!"

Chartres watched Kirkpatrick's hands, and they were gentle as a woman's. Chartres glanced down at his own gloved hands, and a smile grew in his own eyes.

"I think you would prefer, *M'sieur* Kirkpatrick," he said softly, "that this man you hunted *were* your own brother! I think you would relish even that task more than this one!"

151

The limousine plunged into the wreckage—slewed wildly around and heeled over.

Kirkpatrick's voice was harsh. "I perform my duty!" he said shortly.

NITA HEARD these things dimly, almost as if she lay in a trance, but it was not until she was in Kirkpatrick's office that she fully recovered. She sat up then, and groped awkwardly in her pocket for a compact. While the two men watched her intently, she deliberately set about arranging her singed hair, and remedying the damage to her face. She looked up to smile at them brightly.

"Your drivers are very careless, Stanley," she said to Kirkpatrick. "It was only by the greatest luck that I wasn't killed in the explosion that followed the collision!"

Kirkpatrick said, "So that's your story, is it, Nita?"

Nita's violet eyes were very wide. "My story, Stanley? But the evidence is right there! I'm afraid I don't know what you mean. There was a collision, and afterward my car caught fire. The impact must have broken the gasoline line or something. I know the ignition was still turned on."

Nita's smile was stubborn on her lips, but her heart was very heavy. This, she knew, was the end of her efforts to help Dick. She might avoid arrest, but from this time on she would be under surveillance day and night. She could not hope to employ all of Dick's clever methods of evading the police. Was there any way in which she could tell Stanley about the Undertaker? And would his capture help her… help Dick? Stanley was talking….

"I owe this newest Spider a good deal," he said slowly. "Thanks to… him, we captured one of these Bolts and the laboratories are working on it. Only a question of time before we discover

154

how to circumvent it. Also, a number of the Brand's men were removed from the picture permanently. We can identify them easily. I think we may assume that the power of the Brand is broken! And a great part of it is due to this… Spider."

Nita felt pride swell within her at the commissioner's words. If Dick could only know… but Kirkpatrick was wrong, of course. She told him so briefly.

"It is possible that the Brand has been stopped in one more of his ventures," she said quietly, "but that has happened twice before this. Isn't it more likely that he will merely transfer his operations to another field? Oh, Stanley, if you know some of the Brand's men, don't lose any time in tracking down the Brand! I am certain Dick is his prisoner and, after this defeat today—"

"He may take vengeance," Chartres said smoothly, "upon *M'sieur* Wentworth, since he, too, believes him to be the Spider!"

Before Nita could answer, the phone bell on Kirkpatrick's desk whirred, and he snapped it to his ear. "I don't know any John Ramson," he said shortly. "He's what? A radio amateur? A message he has picked up? Oh, well, put him on…."

Nita was sitting suddenly very erectly in her chair, and her eyes were wide. "This is it!" she whispered. It was not a conscious thought. That idea had sprung from somewhere in her subconscious mind. But she knew, she *knew* that somehow Dick….

Kirkpatrick's voice was sharp. "Yes, yes. All right, tell me about it. What sort of a message?" Kirkpatrick was making marks on a pad. Nita stared at them, but they were merely designs. "Confound it, man," Kirkpatrick said sharply. "I don't care about

155

a lecture on the technique of converting a radio receiver into a transmitter.* What is the message?"

Chartres lifted his eyebrows. "These radio amateurs, how do you call them—'hams'? They are all alike. They talk incomprehensible jargon."

But Nita was bending over Kirkpatrick's desk. "Ask him the waveband?" she said, and her voice was edged.

KIRKPATRICK STARED at her, then repeated the question. And at his answer, Nita ran to the radio receiver in a corner of the office and swiftly dialed to the wavelength indicated. There was a long dragging wait while the tubes warmed, and then she heard the awkward, long-drawn signals. It was a painful, howling note on the air, and Nita stared with widening eyes at the transmitter.

"Not sure," she spelled out, "when factory will be destroyed.

---

* AUTHOR'S NOTE: I am not conversant with all the mechanical details of the process of transmitting messages with a radio receiver, but the theory is roughly this: There is a certain circuit in radio hookup which causes the wave impulses, received by the set, to make a second circuit through the identical tubes of the set. This is, I believe, known as a reflex hookup, whereby the same tubes are employed twice so that much greater power is achieved with a minimum of equipment. Sometimes, if the set is not balanced properly, and too much power is thrown into the circuit, the set is said to "heterodyne," which means that the power actually is re-discharged into the atmosphere. Wentworth apparently had either rewired this set, or was fortunate enough to have received one which could be used in this way.

Soon certainly. Clear out all workers. Tell police message from Spider."

Chartres was gazing at her admiringly. "But you can read the International Code!" he exclaimed.

Nita silenced him with an abrupt wave of her hand. "Take this down," she ordered, "as I repeat it. Don't you understand? The Spider is a prisoner of the Brand. Somehow, he has managed to convert a radio receiver into a transmitter. He is risking his life to send this message! Take it down!"

Nita's hands twisted together, but her voice seemed dead calm as she continued to repeat the message which came over the air. Behind her, she could hear Kirkpatrick's voice, crisp with excitement as he called a number on the telephone....

Nita knew a high hope that was strangely compounded with pain. If Dick were free, he would not have had to use this awkward method of communication, depending as it did on the chance that a "ham" would pick it up. If he were discovered in the act....

Nita tried to thrust the thoughts from her mind, to concentrate exclusively on the message.

"Take down very carefully," Wentworth was sending now. "Here is how the Bolt works and how it can be checked. The Bolt concentrates static electricity and discharges it in an instantaneous flame that exhausts the air in any given area, according to how long the Bolt has been focused."

Nita was aware that Chartres wrote rapidly beside her, and Kirkpatrick's voice was lifted angrily, "Damn it, man, I tell you there can be no doubt about it!" he snapped. "The Brand intends to destroy your factory! Get the men out at once! Yes, I know all about your orders, and the size of your staff. About a thousand workers… *They will all be killed unless you order them out!*" Kirkpatrick's voice was silent then, and in the gap, Nita's transliteration went on laboriously, for the sending was painfully slow.

"The method of the Bolt is this…."

Kirkpatrick's voice cut in sharply. "Either empty your shop at once, or I'll dispatch enough men to drive them out. Understand?"

Kirkpatrick slammed up the receiver violently. His heels thudded across the floor toward Nita, but Dick's message had suddenly changed.

"Rush warning!" it howled. "Attack is to…."

The silence was as sudden as a bolt of lightning.

NITA FOUND herself leaning toward the radio, straining with clenched fists, trying to draw some sound from the humming set. Her hand stabbed toward the dial, and she turned it slowly, left and right, hoping against hope. Fear clutched her heart in a cold fist. She spun toward Kirkpatrick.

"They caught him!" she said fiercely. "Don't you understand? They caught him before he could finish that last word! He was telling you that the attack would come tonight, and they caught him. They—"

"Does the Spider mean so much to you?" Chartres asked softly.

Nita spun toward him, and her white fists were lifted. For an instant, her eyes burned into those of the Frenchman, and then she lowered her fists slowly. Her voice was leaden, heavy.

"He is," she said, "the greatest gentleman the world has ever known!"

There was silence in the broad, barren office of Kirkpatrick, silence save for the empty humming of the radio. Kirkpatrick took a step and snapped the switch, and the deeper silence that followed was almost more than could be borne.

Nita shook her head, pressed her wrist to her forehead. "You've got to do something, Stanley," she said heavily. "Those hams may have spotted the direction of the call...."

"We're working on that," Kirkpatrick said softly. "It was the first thing that... the Spider told them to do."

Nita looked up at him, saw the sympathy in his eyes, and her mind snapped back to its normal keenness. She could not betray Dick in this way. She smiled, wanly.

"The Spider has saved my life many times," she said quietly. "If he is a prisoner, I would do anything in my power to save him."

Kirkpatrick nodded, and Chartres watched keenly from a distance. There was still bewilderment in the Frenchman's eyes, but he thought with satisfaction of the cumulative force of the evidence he had got together. Little fragments of suspicious behavior mostly, but he had a great heap of affidavits, and together they were formidable. True, he needed some bit of concrete evidence to complete them, but he was far from despairing. He thought that if the Spider survived the present imbroglio, he would have him by the neck!

"Stanley," said Nita, her voice now stronger, "we'll have to get to that factory right away! God knows what the purpose of its

159

destruction is, but the Spider wouldn't risk his life like that to send a false message. He said... *tonight!*"

"And they caught him at it," Kirkpatrick murmured. "That means it will happen the more quickly. You are right!"

It was less than five minutes later that they were speeding over the Manhattan Bridge across the East River, racing toward the factory. Nita sat rigidly between Kirkpatrick and Chartres, and her eyes burned ahead. Here, she knew, was her greatest hope of grabbing a clue that would lead to the place where Dick was a prisoner. And even that must be done secretly, for if they found Dick captive, and in his cell a radio that would transmit a message such as the Spider had sent....

They were flashing through a lonely district where there were scattered a few dark factories. There were three of the cars; two ahead loaded with heavily armed police. Surely enough to empty the factory in time. She thrust that thought from her mind. Dick had accomplished that purpose all right... if there were no ambush on the way! The Brand would know the police had been warned!

"Stanley!" she cried. "They could ambush us, with the Bolt!"

Kirkpatrick's head whipped toward her, and there was grimness along his jaw. "I know," he said slowly, "but we have no choice."

NITA HELD herself more erectly in the seat, and her chin lifted. Well, Dick was not alone in his danger; those thousand poor workers were not yet safe, thanks to the stubbornness of the fool who directed the plant, who would in his blindness refuse to believe a thing which would cheat him of a few hours' work.

"We've got to get through!" she whispered. "We simply have to!"

Kirkpatrick nodded. Nita's eyes were riveted on his face. That was why she did not see what happened on the road ahead. She didn't see, but she felt the sudden lurch of the limousine, and heard ahead a double, tremendous clap of thunder! Blinding light slashed across her eyes. The shout of the driver was a thin sound on her strained eardrums. The car swerved wildly, and she whipped her gaze ahead. In the road, almost under the front wheels of the wildly swaying limousine, was the wreckage of what had been a car, loaded with armed police. She had only a glimpse of the horror when the limousine plunged into the wreckage, slewed wildly around and heeled over. It smacked on one side, rolled, rolled again. Nita was aware of the violence of the movement, though she was wedged in tightly between the two men, but it was the horror of another thought that strained her eyes so terribly wide. There had been two pitiful heaps of crushed wreckage in the road; two carloads of police had gone to their doom—and there was now no one to bring to safety those thousand doomed souls in the factory!

There was a cry on Nita's lips, and the limousine stopped with a jagged wrench that slammed her violently sideways… and her senses blacked out. When she recovered, she was conscious of movement, of the jouncing of the floor on which she lay, and she realized that she was in a rapidly moving automobile. She moved cautiously, found her hands and ankles firmly bound. She opened her eyes… and light dazzled them. A flashlight was focused on her face.

"Awake, are you?" a man grunted. "Too bad."

Nita could see now that a scarlet robe fell about the man's ankles. She felt fear twist in her vitals, but she made no response, only peered about cautiously. There was another robed man in the driver's seat, and beside him… beside him lolled the inert be-caped figure of—the Spider!

Nita's heart leaped high in her breast as she hungrily studied the outline of the profile above her. This time there could be no mistake. It was Dick! But his head rolled so limply, his whole body was so flaccid. Dear God, had she found him too late? Had they already… taken vengeance? Her hands clenched coldly, and she fought against the terror and the pain within her.

She twisted her head slowly to stare up at the steel mask of the red-robed man. "Is he…" she whispered. "Is he… dead?"

The man guffawed hoarsely. "Dead, no? But he's as good as dead. Drugged to the eyeballs. We're going to plant you all in that factory over there, and then the Brand will pull it down on top of you. It's the boss' idea of a joke."

Nita shuddered, but strangely she was comforted. She realized that it was her faith in Dick that upheld her. So many men had tried to kill him, had sought to make him a helpless sacrifice to their greed—and always he had found a way out. There were times, she realized, when Dick was more than human; times when the great spirit in him could lift him above merely human capability… Master of Men! The smile on Nita's lips was tremulous. She felt… humble. Her eyes rested adoringly on that lolling profile, and a sharp doubt stabbed through her. Drugged. Surely, this was more than even Dick could conquer!

After all, they had held him helpless through the days that had passed, even though he had managed to send out that warning. Nita shook her head. She could not believe that either. If Dick had remained a prisoner of the Brand, it had been for a purpose!

The car lurched to a sudden halt, and the man in red stirred and punched open the door. He caught hold of Nita's ankles and dumped her roughly to the ground, bent over her. She could see the glitter of his eyes through the steel mask's slits, and her flesh shrank. She was glad she had worn a lounge suit.

The man sighed. "Pity to waste something nice like you. But orders is orders."

HE STRAIGHTENED, and Nita heard another car jerk to a halt, heard one man call a greeting. "Them other two is still out cold," he said. "I had to sap Kirkpatrick again."

It was only then that Nita realized that Kirkpatrick and Chartres also were prisoners, that they would share the death that would come with the destruction of the factory. She rolled her head painfully to peer toward the great barren brick building. She was aware now of the hum and champ of its myriad machines, of the harsh lights behind the transomed windows. And then she saw another thing, and she smothered the cry that rose to her lips. Already, there were faint blue flames playing over the metal ventilators on the roof! The Brand had begun his work of destruction!

"We got to hurry," one man growled. "This took a little longer than the Brand said. Monk, stay here and watch the Spider and the dame. We'll take these two punks in first. I wouldn't want Kirkpatrick to miss the fun!"

163

Nita saw that the man who came to stand beside her was the one who had been her captor. She heard him chuckling under the steel mask. "Now ain't that too bad, that I got to watch you?" he whispered.

Nita struggled frantically against her bonds, but they were too tightly knotted. She gathered her strength. Perhaps she could strike with both feet at once... the man was bending over Dick. He drove a violent kick into Dick's side, and there was no stirring in the inert figure, except that one arm jerked limply. Nita set her teeth on her lip, gathered her last reserves of strength. The man was taking off his steel mask.

"Can't properly enjoy things with this mask on," he explained to Nita, and she found herself staring up into the sombre, long face of the killer called the Undertaker. So he was called Monk... He moved toward her, and Nita lashed out with both feet. Her heels only dug into his shins. The man cursed harshly. "I ought to spoil you for that!" he said viciously. He stepped close and lifted a brutal heel over her face.

Nita could not see him, because of that poised foot, but she could look beyond him. She could see... the Spider! Dick was not yet on his feet. He was on his knees, and his head hung like a leaden weight, and there seemed no strength in his movements. His great will was fighting against the drugs, but if this killer turned on him too soon!

"Don't!" Nita whimpered. "Oh, don't do that to me! Do anything else but that!"

The foot moved aside, and she saw the greediness of the eyes that peered down at her. "So, it's like that, is it, you wench?" jeered the Undertaker. "Anything but a bit of face spoiling!"

Nita dared not look again toward where Dick struggled, so pitifully weak, against the drugs. She forced her eyes to cling to those of the man who bent over her. Somehow, she curved her lips into an arch smile.

"Oh, yes," she whispered. "Anything but ruin my looks!"

The Undertaker grunted and bent toward her with marauding hands. "So you're going to be reasonable, are you? I said you was too fancy to waste like that. Imagine a dame like you falling for a dumb egg like the Spider! Why that cheap punk, I could break him with my bare hands!"

The voice that spoke was a little blurred. "Here's your chance, Undertaker," it said. "Like to try your luck with the Spider?"

The man crouched above Nita uttered a strangled oath, and his hand flew toward a holstered gun. Nita saw his face go white with terror, saw the bulging of his eyes. She tried to throw herself against the man's legs, but he had already leaped back. Now at last she could look toward Dick! He stood, stiffly braced, a good dozen feet from her. She could see in his rigidity the effort it cost him even to hold himself erect. And the Undertaker was already snatching out his deadly gun!

WENTWORTH THREW back his head and thin, terrible laughter poured from his lips. He began to walk forward! The lifting of each foot was a powerful effort. But he moved forward, and the laughter continued to pour, dreadfully, from the grim slit of his mouth. The gun in the Undertaker's hand blasted, blasted again… and the Spider did not even waver. The

165

powder-flame threw its red glare across his set face, struck black ridges of shadow across its grim lines, but he did not waver. He came on, slow step after slow step.

Nita, staring at him, felt the terror of that remorseless approach stir coldly within her. This was more than human; this, she felt, was a superman whom nothing could stop! Not even bullets. Not even the Bolt! The Undertaker was trying to steady a hand that shook with the violent tremors of absolute panic. He gripped his trembling hand with his other fist, and the trembling became more violent.

"You're a dead man, Undertaker," said the Spider slowly.

With a scream, the Undertaker whipped back his gun and flung it viciously at Wentworth. The weapon thudded against his chest, dropped to the ground. Wentworth took another slow step forward, and the Undertaker… turned and fled. Screams pumped from his lips. Slowly, Wentworth bent over the gun. His hand groped for it almost blindly, found it. But when his head came up, a fierce directness was in his eyes. The gun suddenly spurted flame.

Nita was not looking toward the Undertaker. Her eyes were wonderingly on the face of the man she loved. Unconsciously, she realized that the screams of the Undertaker had suddenly ceased. She heard a slithering thud on the frozen ground. Now Dick was looking at her, and Dick was smiling, tenderly.

"I knew you'd come, in time," he said, with that same deliberate intonation, while he fought the thickness of his tongue, the paralysis of his throat. "Did you warn the factory?"

Nita's own throat closed. Dick did not yet realize that it was the factory that lifted its black bulk just beyond him. His brain was thickly clouded with the drugs. She bit her lips. She wanted, desperately, not to tell him the truth. He was so weak to fight those men. So weak? Nita laughed sharply. Even this way, the Spider was a match for the Brand and a thousand like him!

"Cut my bonds, Dick," she said clearly. "The factory is here, but the fools inside wouldn't leave! Kirkpatrick and Chartres have been carried unconscious into the building! It will blow up in a moment!"

A spasm seemed to pass across Wentworth's face, left it calm, expressionless. He bent toward Nita, and the bonds painfully cut into her wrists. She saw the powerful arch of his shoulders above her, heard the rasp of his breath. Then the ropes snapped! He laid the captured gun on the ground beside her.

"When the Brand's men return," he said thickly. "Destroy them! There are two bullets left, two of them."

His smile was gentle on his face, but she could see the grimness of his struggle in the white lines about his nostrils, in the firm thrust of his jaw. From beneath his robe, he drew the steel mask of the Spider.

"They equip me well," he muttered. "Guard yourself, my love!" NITA CALLED after him faintly, then set her teeth upon her lips and drew herself erect. Her feet were still bound. She struggled with the bonds, uttering small hopeless sounds that were mingled prayers and sobs. Dick was walking to his doom! That same slow, deliberate lifting of each foot; that laborious progress toward the factory. And her ankles were bound, her fingers numbed from the rope so recently severed from her

167

wrists. She watched Dick go, and calmness came to her slowly. That remorseless majesty of his stride, that slow, fearless advance on certain death! Nita's head lifted with a great pride.

More calmly, she returned to the bonds on her ankles, but when she had got them free, Richard Wentworth had disappeared into the factory. Nita caught up the revolver, and then flung herself prone upon the ground. She, too, had a job to do. Her lips set in resolution!

Above the factory, a desolate siren began to wail. Its note lifted and fell, lifted and fell in the universal signal of disaster. In the factory, men looked up, startled, from their machines; their eyes sought each other and they turned toward the exits, staring. The power of their machines was cut off; the whirring of a thousand wheels was gone. In that unaccustomed silence, men's ears ached with the ululation of the siren.

"Fire signal, Bill!" a man shouted. "We better get the hell out of here!"

The main door of the shop flung open, and a short, irate man strode into the factory.

"Back to your machines!" he snapped. "Who the hell is playing pranks around here? There isn't any fire! Who shut off the power? Turner, throw on the power!"

He rapped out more orders. He did not notice the opening of the door behind him, did not see the caped figure that strode with a ponderous deliberation toward him.

"Be quiet, Hawkins!" said the Spider.

The factory owner whipped around, his face furiously red. He saw the gaunt man in sombre black, stared into the sinister, expressionless face. His hand clawed beneath his coat, whipped out a revolver... and the Spider laughed contemptuously!

"Drop that gun, you fool," he ordered. His voice came out with the same deliberation as his walk. It rang hollowly through the factory, but he scarcely seemed to wait to see that his order was obeyed. He was peering toward the men huddled about their machines.

"In about five minutes," said the Spider steadily, "this place is going to be wrecked by the Brand. Any man within a hundred yards of its walls will be killed. There is plenty of time, if you move swiftly. Simply walk out in double file. You—nearest the door, start. I said *walk!*"

The man who had bolted toward the door checked in mid-stride under the lash of authority. He walked, and behind him the other men moved swiftly in silence. They knew that the Master of Men had spoken.

Not until then did Wentworth turn toward the owner, Hawkins, who stood with the gun hanging from his fingers. Doubt and fear widened his eyes.

"You spoke the truth," he gabbled. "I thought it was a move to scare me. The police... my God! I've got to get out of here!"

"Give me the gun," Wentworth ordered quietly.

Hawkins looked down at the weapon in his hand as if the thing amazed him. His hand trembled. He held it out, snatched his hand from contact with that of the Spider and turned to run.

"Walk!" Wentworth snapped again.

Hawkins checked his dash, and the incipient panic that had stirred among the workers died with his plodding pace. Their

169

faces were pale, but they were calm. One of the older workmen swung a hand gaily toward the Spider.

"Thanks," he said brokenly. "Thanks a lot!"

It was so inadequate. A man laughed, and then another. The line moved more rapidly.

"What's the matter with the Spider?" a man sang out.

And a deep roar answered him. "He's all right!"

BENEATH THE steel mask, Wentworth's lips twisted, though there was warmth in his heart. He stood unmoving, legs braced, back held rigidly. He dared not do anything else. He could scarcely feel the gun in his fingers. All right... as long as his will held firm against the drug. How long its effects would last, he could not guess. More than half the men were already out of the factory.

"March right away from the factory," Wentworth called steadily. "Remember, there's a wide danger zone, and there isn't much time!"

As if to lend point to his words, little blue flames sprang up suddenly on a big slab of steel behind him. It limned his black, gaunt figure, and silence fell upon the men. Their feet shuffled in more rapid tempo. Other equipment was sparking now. Nimble points of blue-white brilliance ran along great wheels, trembled over machines. The harsh work lights were dim by contrast. But the men were already almost out.

Wentworth turned heavily toward the door by which he entered. Somewhere in this building, Kirkpatrick and Chartres lay helpless. He must find them. The sharp crash of a shot came to him dimly from outside, and his lips quivered. Nita had...

destroyed one of the vermin, for there had been no second shot. He pushed open the door and tried to drive speed into his dragging legs. They escaped control, weakened at the knees. He was forced to catch himself against the wall before he could return to his former slow progress.

A light still burned in Hawkins' office. Wentworth stopped outside the door, and a shred of hope sprang up in his chest. Already, he had found Chartres. The flames were inches high on a steel safe when he heaved Chartres to his shoulders and began the crawl toward the exit. How much longer before the building would cave in upon itself? How much longer before the Brand loosed his bolt of destruction? Wentworth did not know, but it was certain it could not be much longer. The static field was building up with incredible rapidity, as the sparkling flames testified.

Chartres was inert across his shoulders, and even the small man's weight was almost more than he could bear. He concentrated not on walking, but on the thought of returning for Kirkpatrick. Somehow with that constant lodestar to guide him, his legs moved more freely. But he was still slow, slow. Would he be able to return in time to save Kirkpatrick? Damn it, he had to! He felt almost a hate for this slight body across his shoulders. Why, in the name of God, had it been Chartres he had found first?

Wentworth pumped his will into the nerve fibres of his body, swung open the door to the outside and began to stagger toward the line of workers that thronged the fields beyond the hundred-yard limit he had set. A cheer went up from them, and suddenly

171

he saw Nita plunging forward. She was alone for a moment, and then two men sprinted after her and raced to relieve him of his burden. Nita's hand was tugging at his arm.

"Oh, hurry, Dick!" she cried. "It will go up at any moment!"

The two men were beside him, lifting Chartres' body from his shoulders. Wentworth did not see Chartres begin to stir slightly as they slung him between them. His eyes were on Nita.

"Get to a phone," he said deliberately. "Call the power company. Find out if there is any heavy drain anywhere in this district, and where it is. If there isn't any, call Equity in New York, and the WPA offices. Find out if any traveling show or carnival is quartered near here for the winter."

Nita nodded eagerly. "Come on, Dick," she whispered. "That building."

WENTWORTH SWUNG about. His eyes saw nothing but her face. He did not see Chartres lift his head and stare toward him as the two men hurried back to the lines.

Wentworth's voice came out weightily. "Kirkpatrick is still inside," he said.

Nita ran to his side. "I'm going with you!"

Wentworth's head swung toward her. "I gave an order," he said flatly.

"To get rid of me!"

"To catch the Brand, my dear," he said. "Go, now. There is little time, so little time!"

Wentworth stalked on, and for a step Nita followed. Her hand stretched out to stop him, yet she knew she could not. Even then, Nita might have disobeyed and followed him into the building that was dancing now with the blue-white fire of destruction. Wentworth looked so small against the bulk of the building; small, yet the dance of his shadow stretched out hugely across the barren field. It was enormous, dominant; a black silhouette of unconquerable power—the will of the Spider!

Nita's fists clenched at her sides. She turned and began to run. "Get away!" she called at the men. "Get at least a half-mile away. The Spider's orders! But leave that man here!"

She pointed imperiously to Chartres, and the men laid him on the earth, and then beat a hasty retreat. To them, the Spider's orders had become law… and it was the dictates, too, of their own sense of self-preservation. Nita stood above the limp form of Chartres while the men hurried away. Her lips were drawn tight.

"If he has to die," she said flatly, "you will not escape, *M'sieur* Chartres!"

An instant longer she stood there, and then she darted away to find the telephone and make the calls Wentworth had ordered, but her heart was heavy within her. She was so terribly afraid. She dared not look again toward the factory, but the weird blue light danced ahead of her on the uneven ground as she ran. Behind her, Chartres lifted his head. There was pure bewilderment in his eyes, but he lay there, motionless, staring up at the black arch of the sky, the weird flicker of blue.

He was still there when a great shout lifted over the fields, a muffled, rising cheer that went on and on without end. It was only then that he moved. He saw then why they shouted. Out of the door of the factory staggered the Spider, and across his shoulders was the inert form of Commissioner Kirkpatrick! They were almost upon Chartres, and he reeled to his feet as they passed. He got his shoulder under Kirkpatrick's thighs and helped to carry him along.

Curiously, Chartres heard whispered words that came from behind the Spider's mask, but he knew instantly that they were not addressed to him. The Spider did not even seem aware of his presence, of his assisting shoulder beneath Kirkpatrick's thighs.

"Weakling!" Wentworth taunted himself. "Why are you staggering? A trifling wound in your leg? A little drug in your blood? Weakling! This is not the end! The Brand, you fool, you weakling! The Brand! You'll know where he is soon, and then... and then...."

The monologue went on and on, driven by an inexhaustible will. Chartres felt the pull of that will, as he strode beside the Spider toward the cheering crowd. He felt the enormity of the effort it required for this man even to place one foot before the other. Once Wentworth stumbled and would have fallen but for Chartres' suddenly braced arm about him.

Wentworth stood stock-still a moment, shuddered, then stumbled on. His voice was silent, but the struggle of that mighty will within him dragged him on remorselessly. Chartres matched his stride. They were a hundred and fifty yards from the factory walls now; perhaps more. It was still a long way to the cheering ranks of the crowd. A long way....

Suddenly, Chartres was fighting against a howling gale. It tore his clothing from his shoulders, drove him backward two full paces before he could begin to brace himself. With a stran-

174

gled shout in his throat, he realized what was happening. He contrived to throw himself against Wentworth's legs, flinging him and his burden to earth. The Spider lay still as death.

Chartres did not know how long he lay there motionless under the brutal assault of the winds. The rumble of the thunder that followed stopped his ears completely, so that he heard no sound at all… and when he staggered to his feet, the factory was a heap of wreckage. He stood very silent and peered down at the still figure of the Spider, his head pillowed on the chest of Kirkpatrick, the man he had saved. Strangely, there was mockery in the eyes of Raoul Chartres. Here they lay, two great enemies… perhaps two great friends. And the head of one was pillowed upon the chest of the other.

Chartres laughed. He shook his head as he bent toward them, *"Eh bien, mon vieux,"* he murmured. "You who mocked me and said I would not catch the Spider. You are at my mercy, is it not so?"

THE CROWD had vanished in terror when Nita came racing back across the fields. She searched in vain for any sight of Dick, and a great anger surged through her. This was a thing that could not happen, but it had occurred many times in the past. The people whom the Spider saved could cheer him when they were out of danger. They would not dare even the smouldering ruins to make sure of his life!

She raced on, breath sobbing in her throat, and then suddenly she saw Wentworth and Kirkpatrick in a huddle upon the ground. She flung herself down on her knees, and her voice was urgent as she spoke Dick's name. It seemed impossible that he should hear her in the depths of the stupor of drugs and wound and exhaustion which had claimed him. Nothing but Nita's voice could have reached his mighty will. He heard her and he heeded. Slowly, the will stirred within him, and he opened his eyes; he lifted his head.

Nita's hand under his arm urged him to his feet, and he stared back at the ruins of the factory, then down at Kirkpatrick on the ground.

"He isn't hurt," Nita told him quickly. "Just knocked out. Come, Dick, let's get away from here at once!"

"Chartres?" Wentworth said thickly.

"You brought him out first," Nita cried. "Oh, hurry, Dick!"

Wentworth nodded, and his hands reached up to grip his temples, encountered the steel mask. "I thought I had saved Chartres first, too," he said, "but coming from the building, I had the strangest feeling that he was with me—helping me!"

Nita laughed scornfully. "Chartres helping you? Come, Dick! If Stanley should recover his senses, you would be doomed!"

Wentworth nodded ruefully. "Yes. I must go. What did you find out, Nita, about the electric power and the carnival?"

Nita sucked in a slow, weary breath. She had hoped he might forget… "No electric drain," she said slowly. "Over the hill there, as nearly as I can figure from what I was told, there is a carnival holed up for the winter. An old farm building, with barns, where they keep the animals. They have menagerie shows sometimes even in winter, when the weather permits it, and… Dick, where are you going?"

Wentworth's voice came back thinly: "I am going to 'snatch a

Brand from the burning,'" he quoted. "I think my methods will be surer than the electric chair!"

Nita ran after him, but he sent her remorselessly back. "I'm all right now, dear," he said, "and you can't afford to have Kirkpatrick know you went off with… the Spider! Tell him, when he revives, where I have gone! To put an end to a carnival of murder!"

The distance was interminable, and the hill seemed too steep for any mortal to climb. But Wentworth kept stolidly on, and there was a fierce and consuming anger in his breast. Over the hill there, he would find the Brand, if he moved swiftly enough. This time, the Brand had betrayed himself. He had made an attack in a locality where the drain of the huge machine required for such a major destruction, by contrast with the small, pre-charged Bolt which killed men, would definitely register on the light system of the city. Failing that, he would have to have a portable dynamo—and there was only one sort of business that used them to any extent. Besides, Wentworth knew that the Brand had once been connected with a carnival. A fire-eater in the freak show….

Relentless as death itself, the Spider climbed the hill.

HE PASSED over its crest, and his eyes were turned toward the clustered, slattern buildings at the foot of the hill when, behind him, a man giggled!

"No, just stand like that, Spider," came the voice. "I want to talk to you a little while before I break your spine with a bullet. The Bolt would be too kind to you!"

Wentworth drew to a weary halt, and there was satisfaction

in his heart, for the voice was the voice of the Brand! He had been right. He had found his prey. It only remained to… snatch the Brand from the burning.

Wentworth laughed a little. The sound of it was odd. He felt light-headed, but there was a deadly seriousness in his heart. For the first time, a doubt assailed him. He was so confident of destroying the Brand… but the man had a gun at his back!

"Funny," said the Spider, and his voice sounded silly and a little mad. "Very funny. I came to snatch a brand from the burning, and now I'm going to get burned down myself! Isn't it funny, Bosher?"

The Brand swore harshly. "So you know me, Spider!" he snapped. "How in the hell did you know it?"

Wentworth swung around heavily. He removed his steel mask, and his face seemed vapid. "Know what?" he asked thickly. "These damned drugs you gave me… can't seem to hear right."

Bosher came forward two slow steps. He wore the scarlet robe, the expressionless mask. "How many others know who I am?" he demanded harshly.

Wentworth smiled slowly. "Oh, lots of people," he said. "It was very simple, though I didn't know entirely until I found out that a carnival power plant was being used. You used to be a fire-eater in a sideshow, Bosher. I began to suspect you when you so openly made an ally of Blinky McQuade. And you overpaid for the job, Bosher. Crooks don't deal as openly as that, and you know it, and Blinky McQuade was supposed to talk too much. Some people even suspect him of being a stool pigeon to the police. So you made a partner of Blinky McQuade, who is a known coward about guns, so that the news that you were against the Brand would get back to the police. That was enough to make me suspicious, Bosher.

"And then, too, you hated me so thoroughly, Bosher, and though all crooks hate the Spider, you have an especial reason to dislike him. He gave you that stiff ankle, Bosher, by smashing it with a bullet, long ago!"

Bosher swore. "So you are Blinky McQuade, too, are you, Spider?"

Wentworth laughed emptily. "Funny, isn't it? But then that will do me no more good. You're going to kill me, aren't you, Bosher? That's all right, too, but I'm glad you're wearing a mask, Bosher. I'd hate to see that ugly face of yours gloating over me when you shoot!"

Bosher giggled behind his mask. "Hate that, would you, Spider?"

Wentworth said, "Damn you! You're not going to gloat over me!"

Bosher's hand went up to the mask. It was a thing only a madman would have risked against the Spider, but then he thought that the Spider was fuddled with drugs; and he hated the Spider with a deadly intensity. He jerked at his mask, and for an instant he could not see clearly. It was then that Wentworth flung his own heavy steel mask and hurled himself forward!

His mask sailed straight and cupped over the muzzle of the gun, even as Bosher, recovering himself with a wild shout, squeezed the trigger! The bullet clanged on the steel, sent the mask spinning, but before he could shoot a second time, the Spider was upon him!

WENTWORTH'S LEFT hand clamped down on the gun wrist and bore it toward the earth, and the fingers of his right hand clamped hard about Bosher's throat.

"They should always hang cowardly killers, Bosher," Wentworth said coldly. "Burning is too good for them. Far too good!"

His fingers tightened inexorably....

When Bosher hung, a dead and lifeless weight from his grasping hand, Wentworth let go and watched the limp body of the Brand slide to the earth. He stood swaying on his feet then. He dragged a hand across his brows. So great a struggle... the strength was gone from him. He fumbled with his pocket and somehow managed to get out his cigarette case. He bent and pressed the base against the forehead of the dead man. He tried to straighten, and he could not. The strength was not in him.

Furiously, his will fought to command his body. He had told Nita to bring the police, and they would be here soon. But for once, his magnificent body refused to answer the summons of his valiant will. There was no call to duty, no service to humanity to urge him on now. His task was finished; the Brand was dead. Self-preservation was not as great an urge to this patriot of the world as was the call of duty.

So Wentworth fought to save himself, and the effort did not seem worthwhile. He got one foot on the ground, and he achieved no more. It was then that a figure in a red robe darted out of the underbrush and raced forward with a leveled gun! Wentworth saw the man and realized only then that there remained one killer unaccounted for when the factory had smashed. This was he, then. This was the end. Wentworth pitched forward ahead of the blast of the gun. He sagged down into the grateful darkness of unconsciousness while the man in red still rushed toward him....

Nita worked frantically over Kirkpatrick. He had been struck heavily over the head, and his scalp was cut and swollen. At last he revived, and hearing Nita's message from the Spider, he rose. Together, they started on a stubborn run toward the carnival farm over the hill. They burst over the crest, and two men in red robes lay dead there, and on one of them there burned the scarlet seal of the Spider. There was no one else in sight until they heard a cry from the carnival buildings.

"*Hola!*" a man called. "*Hola!* I say—I've found Wentworth!"

Kirkpatrick's head snapped about, and he saw the small, dapper figure of Chartres outlined against the dull light that shone from the open door of one of the barns. Nita began to run toward the barn before the words had more than reached them, and Kirkpatrick raced in her wake. His long strides ate up the distance, and his lips were very grim. If Chartres had found Wentworth... then this was the end. There was grief in his heart but no swerving in his loyal mind. The Commissioner of Police was a man who knew his duty and performed it without fear or favoritism.

Nita was only a pace ahead of him as she burst into the barn. She ran immediately to where Wentworth lay, swathed in ropes that were knotted time and time again. His eyes were open now, and there was a smile on his lips as Nita bent toward him.

Chartres said gravely to Kirkpatrick, "I thought I should leave him as I found him until you arrived! My friend, after that explosion on the road, I did not expect to see you alive again! *Ma fois!* A marvelous man, this Spider! He cleared the factory, carried me out, returned and carried you out also, just before the factory collapsed. A truly marvelous man—saving his enemies!" **KIRKPATRICK NODDED** moodily, and his eyes rested on Nita and Wentworth. He watched Nita's nimble hands untying the ropes.

"I'm sorry to find you... alive, Dick," he said slowly.

Nita gasped, and spun toward him. Chartres' brows lifted. He slowly lighted a cigarette.

Kirkpatrick nodded and said, "I have to arrest you, Dick," he said heavily, "on charges of murder, and on charges of being the Spider. Chartres has complete evidence, and I have warned you that when the evidence came into my hands, I would act!"

Wentworth nodded. "Quite right, too," he agreed. "Though I'll confess, I am curious to learn what this evidence against me is."

Nita wrenched the last of the ropes free from about Dick, and then she jumped to her feet. "You are mad!" she cried. "You are a graceless clown!" She stamped her foot. "How *dare* you, Stanley Kirkpatrick, after he has saved your life...."

"Your pardon, *ma'mselle,*" Chartres murmured. He had the cigarette going, and the blue smoke clouded his face. "Your pardon, but it was not this Wentworth who saved the Commissioner. It was the Spider. With my own eyes, I saw it!"

Kirkpatrick whipped about, his eyes narrow. "Say that again," he demanded roughly.

Chartres shrugged delicately, waved a careless hand. "First, I want to make the little speech," he said. "After I was carried from the factory building, I revived to find myself alone. I saw the Spider come from the building, carrying you on his shoulders, my friend. So I help him just a little bit, for the Spider seems tired.

"I am jubilant. I say to myself, 'But this is too easy, Raoul!' I have only to put the handcuffs on this Spider, and he is mine! So soon, of course, as he has carried you, *M'sieur* Kirkpatrick, to safety!"

"You're a callous beast!" Nita cried.

"I, too, have a duty!"

"Quiet, Nita," Wentworth said gently. "He is entirely right." Now Chartres had him dead to rights. A while ago, Wentworth had dropped unconscious while a man in red raced to kill him, and he awoke to find himself wrapped in rope like a cocoon, while Chartres shouted at the door.

"Unfortunately—" Chartres drew another cigarette and lighted it from the first. "Unfortunately, there is this implosion just when I think things are ready, and I succumb. I lie there upon the ground beside this Spider and the man he has saved. I, who was so eager and ready to make the arrest, thwarted by the very blast from which this same man saved me."

Kirkpatrick said vehemently, "I'm still waiting for an explanation. You had evidence. Now suddenly—"

"You are impatient, *M'sieur* Kirkpatrick," Chartres complained. "Me, I like a good story!"

"Let him go on, Kirk," Wentworth said quietly. "After all, there is no hurry."

"No," agreed Chartres amiably, "for this same Spider has killed the Brand. I saw it—I! With these very eyes! With one hand, he holds down the Brand's so-deadly gun. With the other… he squeezes, very slowly, this Brand to death!" Chartres clamped his hand about his throat by way of demonstration. His eyes bulged. He freed his throat, cleared it a little. "It was very dramatic."

"Very," Kirkpatrick agreed quietly.

CHARTRES LIFTED his eyebrows at him and began to fumble for another cigarette. "Just then, this other figure in red dashes from the underbrush, and the Spider takes up the dead man's gun. Pouf! Another enemy is slain. Remarkable, this Spider! Figure for yourself my position! I am here ready to make the arrest! The Spider is before me, weak from fighting!

"True, the Spider is an excellent shot—but he does not shoot the police!" Chartres gestured widely with both hands. "What would you do? It is not brave, *non*, to hold a gun on a man who will not shoot you? And yet, there is my duty. I reach into my pocket for my so able gun… and behold, it is not there!"

"Still," Kirkpatrick's noted acidly, "you could bluff this man who could not use a gun against you!"

"That is what I think," admitted Chartres gravely. "I challenge him… and identify myself of course. He turns, and I see his face… and then he laughs at me! He laughs, do you understand, *messieurs, et ma'mselle?* And me, I can do nothing! It is paralyzing, that laughter. And the Spider, he turn and run away from me. Before I can recover, he had disappear' over the hill!"

"Toward the barn, you mean!" Kirkpatrick snapped.

"Not at all, *m'sieur,*" Chartres said gently. "Over the hill! But I find it strange, *M'sieur le Commissionaire,* that you wish to arrest this man who you say has saved your life!"

Kirkpatrick said angrily, "This is enough of quibbling. I have my duty, and I perform it! You saw the face of the Spider! Identify him!"

Chartres turned his expressionless face toward Wentworth, and Nita's arms tightened about Wentworth's neck. Chartres bowed gravely. "On the contrary, *m'sieur,* I must tell you that it was not this Wentworth. It is a man I never saw before!"

"Your evidence!" Kirkpatrick rasped.

Chartres snapped his fingers. "Before the evidence of my eyes, it vanishes like that. *M'sieur* Wentworth, I owe you an apology, as well as thanks... for some pleasant maneuvers!"

Wentworth bowed. "You, sir, saved my life... from the Brand!"

"Enfin!" Chartres struck his hands together. "We are even, then, eh? *M'sieur le Commissionaire,* I wish to tender my resignation, effective at once. A life is precious, is it not, and I cannot further hunt this Spider, for you see... he saved this worthless life of mine!"

Kirkpatrick said flatly, "There is still duty!"

"And patriotism, *m'sieur!*" Chartres returned. "As I believe you were once so kind as to point out to me. You called it, I believe, a higher patriotism, a service to the humanity! A big task! Much

185

too great for me, who may only do some little thing for France, perhaps!"

Kirkpatrick's smile came reluctantly to his stiff lips. He held out his hand. Impulsively, Nita ran forward to hold out her own. Chartres clicked his heels together, lifted that fragile hand to his lips.

"It has been a pleasure," he murmured. *"Fois de gentilhomme!"*

And as he strolled in his careless way out through the door, Chartres turned and winked—deliberately.

"Faith of a gentleman," Nita whispered to Wentworth. "I perceive that a gentleman must also know when to… lie!"